DEPTH OF REVENGE

By Richard Golden

iUniverse, Inc.
New York Bloomington

Depth of Revenge
A Novel

iUniverse books may be ordered through booksellers or by contacting:

iUniverse
1663 Liberty Drive
Bloomington, IN 47403
www.iuniverse.com
1-800-Authors (1-800-288-4677)

Because of the dynamic nature of the Internet, any Web addresses or links contained in this book may have changed since publication and may no longer be valid. The views expressed in this work are solely those of the author and do not necessarily reflect the views of the publisher, and the publisher hereby disclaims any responsibility for them.

ISBN: 978-1-4401-1525-7 (pbk)
ISBN: 978-1-4401-1527-1 (cloth)
ISBN: 978-1-4401-1526-4 (ebk)

Library of Congress Control Number: 2009922572

Printed in the United States of America

iUniverse rev. date: 3/6/2009

To my parents

CHAPTER 1:
IRONICALLY, THE NAME OF MY BOAT MEANS "REVIVAL"

They are about to attack us. The pings of active sonar increase in intensity. I doubt its source is Iranian or Arab. I hope it does not foreshadow another attack by a Western navy. I miss the crewman who gave his life in the last attack. I hear unsecured equipment that threatens to reveal our position. I blame the intelligence officer we took onboard midway through our mission. Voices call out damage reports, but the language uses a code I cannot understand. I feel the pressure of the equipment that scans my iris to confirm my identity before we can launch nuclear-tipped missiles. The light grows intense. Something is wrong. The inside of a submarine can't grow bright.

Slowly, conscious sensations replace my misinterpretations. I realize the sonar sound is the patient monitor. The clang of the unsecured equipment turns into meal trays loaded into a cart, and damage reports repeatedly summon a doctor in German-accented English. The pressure against my eye is applied by my uncomfortable sleep position that fails to blot out the morning sun. I start to remember. Our nuclear-tipped cruise missiles have either been launched or lie at the bottom of the sea.

Every sensation confirms my conclusion that I'm not aboard my submarine. I feel relief that I'm not in the kind of danger I've dreamed.

But I'm disappointed to remember that I'm under guard within an American military hospital in Germany. I expect to receive more treatments soon to alleviate my radiation sickness. I can then anticipate more interrogation sessions with American military intelligence officers. I expect the questions will scrutinize my actions in response to my final written orders. The orders take the form of a letter. The final page of the letter taken from me by one of their submariners a few days ago reads, "We know you will uphold the highest traditions of our nation and our people." The signature belongs to the prime minister of Israel.

I'm sure my interrogators have come to appreciate that I give them complete answers, even if my explanations suggest I've made poor decisions. I look forward to the chance to analyze my decision-making process and find logical reasons for my choices. Most of all, I also will have the opportunity to take pride in the outstanding performance of my crew under very trying circumstances.

There is a Hebrew word *Tekumah*. The word denotes the concept of "renewal" or "revival." It refers to the rebirth of the Jewish people after the Holocaust following the establishment of Israel. It also describes the painfully slow recovery process in Israel that I see on television.

What is certain, though, is that *Tekumah* is the name of the Israeli submarine aboard which I, Gilad, served in the capacity of the final commanding officer.

* * *

I didn't grow up intending to perform my service obligation

with the navy or to serve such a long career as a member of the Israeli Defense Forces. When my vision fell below Israeli Air Force standards, I tested for and passed the qualification examinations for the Israeli Sea Corps. I liked it well enough to make it my career.

All nations' submariners deserve the moniker of the "silent service." With the fame of Israel's soldiers and pilots, our service is especially "silent" in comparison to our ground and air forces. So I should tell you about my crew even before I describe my boat. Like all Israeli submarine crews, we are often known by the nickname "force 700," in reference to the average score prospective crew members received on an intelligence test. Reportedly, this score translates to an equivalent IQ of 130 to 140.

I'm in charge of thirty-two officers and men. We also berth four men who are special officers. They are not considered combat officers. You'll appreciate the irony in this classification later.

Our boat can carry a combination of sixteen torpedoes and cruise missiles for use in our ten forward-facing tubes. Four of the tubes can accommodate the Popeye Turbo Missiles. The other six are for the Harpoon missiles or torpedoes. For this mission, our ordnance consists of ten Popeye Turbo missiles, four Harpoons, and two torpedoes. Both types of cruise missiles are nuclear capable.

My cabin is extremely cramped. Even without the dangers aboard and the risk of death from the crushing pressure and hostility of the ocean, there would be protests should a prisoner serve his sentence in such confinement. Of course, I don't spend a lot of time there. Yet even this small cabin has much more room and privacy than the triple bunks provided for most of the rest of the crew. Their space resembles the famous photograph of the boys and men peering out of their bunks at a Nazi concentration camp.

The boat I command was built in Germany. She represents

the last of three *Dolphin*-class diesel-electric submarines built in Germany for the Israeli Sea Corps. In a funny way, Israel can thank the late Saddam Hussein for these boats. When the Americans launched their first war against Iraq, Israelis, including my family, huddled in bomb shelters and safe rooms. Israelis took refuge out of fear of the Scud missiles Iraq launched toward our cities. Those missiles, equipped with warheads partially developed by German firms, terrorized us with the fear that they contained German-developed chemical weapons. German officials decided the right thing to do would be to pay for two submarines. Sometimes, we call them the "Saddam" and the "Hussein." Israel paid for *Tekumah*.

Our boat served a variety of missions in her first years of service. We trailed weapons-carrying ships, offloaded special forces troops, and patrolled the coastal waters near Israel, Syria, Lebanon, Gaza, and Egypt.

If you are an American who studied or lived through the cold war, you already know the reason submarines are a critical component of national defense. You deployed thousands of nuclear weapons for use by hundreds of land-based missiles and bombers. However, the missile silos were fixed at known locations. The bombers required time to take off and fly to a safe distance from their bases. You wanted a fleet of submarines undetectable to the Soviets. Your submarine fleet provided deterrence against any surprise attack. The Soviets might get the idea that they could catch all your missiles in their silos and shoot down your bombers or destroy them in their hangers or on the runway. They certainly never imagined they could sink most of your submarines. They knew that those remaining submarines could launch enough ballistic missiles to destroy them. You called this "deterrence" or "second strike" capability.

Even more than the Americans, Israel needs deterrence. Our enemies do not lay halfway around the globe. They are either on or near our borders. Our leaders worry principally regarding the intentions of Iran. You might remember the estimate from the American intelligence agencies that Iran likely suspended the weapon component of its nuclear program in 2003. Converting enriched nuclear materials into a nuclear weapon is a process that can be reactivated quickly. Our intelligence services believe the Iranian leadership decided to suspend certain processes in order to prevent discovery of Iran's intent to produce a weapon. The difficult part of creating the weapon is production of enough sufficiently enriched material for a bomb. So even after the suspension of the program, thousands of gas centrifuges continued in operation. There is no purpose for this processing; all Iran's requirements for the nuclear fuel for its energy programs are to be supplied under the terms of its agreement with Russia. Iran also maintains a heavy water reactor that produces plutonium that is not suitable for reactor fuel but is ideal for fabricating a plutonium nuclear weapon. You might also wonder why Iran needs a nuclear energy program with the amount of oil reserves under its soil and why it invested in nuclear technology instead of addressing its shortage of gasoline refineries. You also might speculate why Iran purchased Russian ballistic missiles from North Korea with a design specifically to carry nuclear warheads and built hardened silos for these missiles. Our prime minister does not enjoy the luxury of speculating.

Israel is approximately the size of New Jersey, and our missile launchers and air bases may not be sufficiently hardened against nuclear attack. So our enemies might imagine they could destroy all our air bases and missile launchers, leaving our armed forces powerless to retaliate against them. This vulnerability is also dangerous for our adversaries. The systems we employ to detect and track missile launches are of the highest technology. However, with the threats coming from such close distances, the time between our detection of a ballistic missile attack and its arrival would be less than fourteen minutes. If our prime minister faced the possibility of destruction of the land-based missiles, his reaction to such a notification might be to "use them or lose them." Our risk of loss of these ground-based weapons would make us more likely to launch a strike without confirmation of the nature of an attack against us. When one or more of our submarines are deployed with nuclear-tipped missiles, the prime minister knows that our retaliatory ability is not contained in a nation ten miles across in places, but somewhere unknown to our enemies in the open seas. So our survivable submarine deterrent actually protects our enemies against our miscalculation of the certainty of an attack, its launch point, trajectory, or its likely payload.

Newspapers reported in May 2000 that Israeli *Dolphin*-class submarines tested the Popeye Turbo missile in the waters off Sri Lanka and hit a target fifteen hundred kilometers downrange. These missiles suffer disadvantages compared with the missiles carried in the American ballistic missile submarines. Aside from the shorter range, they fly much slower and can be shot down by a modern air defense. Their payload is much smaller. However, they enjoy an accuracy advantage in that they remain guided all the way to the target. Of course, accuracy might not be so important depending upon the designated target and the payload of the missile.

Before you start to worry, let me assure you that submarine commanders are authorized to fire the missiles upon approval of only four people: the prime minister, the defense minister, the chief of staff of the Israeli army, and the commander of the navy. Of course, we utilize alternate procedures should this group be knocked out.

Most of the time one of our *Dolphin*-class submarines patrols the Mediterranean Sea. A second boat often cruises the Red Sea, the Gulf of Oman, or occasionally, the Persian Gulf. The third faces maintenance, crew training, or standby duty.

I need to explain how our boat functions. She operates in a way that bears resemblance to the hybrid car your neighbor drives. She always uses an electric motor for propulsion. She uses batteries to power the motor. If our batteries' condition permits, she should remain fully submerged for the most stealth.

The rate at which the submarine exhausts the energy stored in her batteries depends primarily upon the level of power applied to the boat's propulsion. If we choose to cruise at a minimal pace, the charge will last for several days. Should we need to achieve our maximum speed, *Tekumah* could not maintain such a pace for even an hour before the batteries' charge would be completely depleted.

Most days we must operate her diesel motors once or twice in order to recharge the batteries. At that time the diesel motor also provides the electricity to run the electric motor. Those motors need air to breathe, so the submarine must ascend close enough to the surface of the ocean that our snorkels can pierce the surface. We can then take in air for and vent exhaust gases from the motors. Of course, then our submarine is not so invisible.

If you stood next to me now, you would first notice the odor of diesel fumes, battery acid, and body odor. The submarine manufactures oxygen through electrolysis of water. However, we must maintain a lower than normal oxygen level to reduce the possibility of a fire. The boat also uses "scrubbers" to remove some of the carbon dioxide from our air. No device removes the odor. *Tekumah* does not produce enough water from our reverse osmosis unit or distillers for regular or long showers. On the other hand, usually we are too busy or tired for even short ones. With all of the odors in our environment, we really don't notice our own stink. Once, at the start of a port call to Turkey, the crew stood on the dock next to each other. Yosef commented how much Turkey smelled like body odor.

You might wonder where I learned my English. My mother, who runs the business office of one of Haifa's largest law firms, forced her children to learn English. She grew up in California before moving to Israel as a teenager. Even though her Hebrew is very good, she spoke almost exclusively in English inside our home. I also attended UCLA for my graduate studies in engineering.

My father owns an automotive repair facility. Both of my siblings are dead. One died while performing military service in Lebanon and the other in a car crash. I have never married, and I have no children.

I cannot be sure of my crew's thoughts regarding my tenure as their commander. I think they appreciate that I stand up for them. When Boris's consumption of a bodybuilding supplement caused him to fail a drug test, I persuaded the authorities to order him reinstated to the crew. I also fought unsuccessfully for Yuri's promotion in recognition of his time-consuming evaluation of the boat's array of multiple-spectrum digital cameras that supplement our optical periscope. I think what they really appreciate about me is that I forced the transfer of the previous executive officer. He triggered unrest with the crew and then made my job harder than it needed to be. First, he needlessly removed the last bits of privacy from the crew in the name of efficiency and discipline. He had to know the subject of every conversation on the boat. Second, he never learned that "if everything is important, then nothing is important." He always reported every minor rule's transgression to me.

Israeli submariners are a lot more disciplined than those of most other nations' navies. We don't often get into bar fights with crewmen of rival submarines or surface vessels, "surface targets," according to our slang.

Of course, we permit some forms of pranks, within reason. It is a matter of weighing the morale boost of the prankster and his cohorts against the feelings of the "victim." For example, a junior officer is often targeted by a group of enlisted men. One member of the group is designated the "Mossad" officer. His assignment will be to surreptitiously add the emblem of the navy chief of staff to a junior officer's uniform. The crew then caters to the officer in accord with the protocols required for the presence of such a dignitary. Such royal treatment lasts until he notices or asks why he commands such attention. There would be no reason for the victim to feel upset concerning his failure to notice the change to his uniform or being singled out for extra attention.

I do impose several extra rules on my boat. Wives and girlfriends must stay out of visual range of the gate at our base in Haifa. If the men must engage in emotional good-byes, they should do it privately and not compete with each other. I also maintain rules governing moments when the men must urinate while on duty. They must use one of those plastic containers provided to hospital patients who cannot leave their bed. There is too great a chance of spillage when the man employs a container that does not seal. Otherwise the rules on my boat are identical to those enforced on the other two submarines.

I welcome the crew back aboard for our next mission. The men stow their gear and perishable food and perform final equipment checks. They still find a moment to compare DVD titles of the discs they bring, discuss capacities and capabilities of their MP3 players, and show off pictures of family and girlfriends.

The special officers arrive last and in one group. They hold lower ranks than I do, but in the IDF, salutes are the exception. I know Israelis behave impolitely, but in this case, it is a matter of how busy our mission keeps us. The special officers take their orders directly from Tel Aviv. The assignment of such specialists to our boat was inaugurated the moment we started to carry nuclear weapons. They are present to both prevent unauthorized use and enable authorized use of these weapons. When they were assigned aboard *Tekumah*, my superior officer explained to me that I should compare the arrangement with that between an anesthesiologist and a surgeon.

"One doctor did not outrank the other, and both positions contributed equally to the success of the operation," he said.

The special officers used a fishing trip analogy where the crew represented the children who rowed the boat and could throw rocks, but they controlled use of the fishing gear. I think our crew respects them according to how well they perform during firefighting and emergency drills. I hope they are never needed, or they, along with the rest of the crew, probably won't have any reason to return home.

The special officers also perform another important function. They serve in the capacity of communications officers for all nontactical communication. This responsibility involves oversight of the communication between the crew and home. We operate equipment that enables several means of communication. First, we broadcast and receive across several bands of radio frequencies. Several of the bands operate underwater when the submarine extends a long thin line. We also access the Internet. Now I don't think I'm giving the bad guys any ideas they haven't thought of. Let me say that if you open an e-mail account and save your writing in the form of a draft, it avoids the Internet service provider's eyes and filters. The person who reads the message needs only the account name and password. Each crew member receives a message about once a week from only one contact per person. That person is evaluated and cleared by the security services who then instruct them regarding permissible topics for communication. The communication flows only one way; the crew cannot make contact back home. If I think the news should wait until the crew returns home, for example, death or divorce, I'm allowed to hold the message or even modify it.

As is our boat's tradition, I'll only brief the men after we get well under way. Of course, when they notice the extra boxes on the floors, the soft bags attached to the sides of the passageways, and the shower filled with more boxes, they know our mission will last for at least forty days.

We pull out of our pen at our Haifa base at night. Our command strives to make it difficult for anyone to determine whether the submarine fleet remains in port or is deployed at sea. When the submarine is in port, we may not answer phone calls from unidentified sources. This prohibition prevents an intelligence agency from easily determining our boat's presence in port by simply placing a few phone calls.

We cruise out to deep water to perform our trim dive. We must make sure that both the front and back of the boat are not too heavy or too light. We must make this adjustment periodically throughout our mission because we consume fuel and supplies. On one occasion a crew member of another submarine arranged a "trim party." The organizer herded a group of men from the bow to the stern and back to make it tough to set the boat's trim correctly. The organizer and even "the sheep" faced discipline. Word of the incident reached the other submarine crews, so our men remain at their normal stations during this procedure.

Next, we dive to a depth sufficient to put the boat under approximately 90 percent of the rated pressure. We discover, to no one's surprise, only a few minor drips, and the leaking flanges are easily tightened.

When Erez tightens the flanges, he makes our boat's traditional comment.

"Billions of shekels for our house—and the roof leaks."

We perform an "up and down bubbles." This operation places the boat at extreme up-and-down angles. The exercise permits us to discover anything that might break free under such radical angles. The assurance that we stand a better chance of staying quiet while on patrol outweighs the momentary unpleasantness.

I know other nations' navies attempt to track us, so I follow a procedure to depart from base that attempts to minimize our submarine's risk of detection. I won't give you much detail, but I can say that, in general terms, if a submarine travels underneath or behind another noisy vessel, it makes it harder to track the submarine for that period of time. Our course is a special kind of zigzag. I employ different methods to randomize the course but keep our general direction of travel. I can roll dice or flip pages of a book and use the result for a variation. For instance, if I roll two dice and they show three and four and I flip the pages of my book and it lands on page 567, then I might vary the course for thirty-four minutes by 5.67 degrees. Obviously, if this method produces a result that doesn't make sense, then I repeat my procedure or modify it. The point is that no one knows what our exact heading or position will be even several minutes in the future. Our navigation is really not much of an issue. We can double-check our position through use of the GPS (global positioning satellite) system when we are near the surface, but we are never far off.

I must speak to the men soon and brief them regarding our mission. I want the men assigned to the second watch to get their sleep. Only the benefits of the exhaustive work schedule enable decent sleep aboard a submarine. There is much motion as well as noise from crew communications and activities. The most you can do sometimes is to lie quietly, wearing an eye mask and earplugs. My cabin has a redundant set of several of the boat's important gauges. The convenient display allows me to avoid bothering the crew to obtain assurance of the details the gauges provide.

I set the communications system to "all compartments" and inform the crew what I can about our mission. We all expect to patrol the Mediterranean. Instead, *Tekumah* is to sail to a rendezvous with a cargo ship in the South Atlantic Ocean, near South Africa. For security purposes, headquarters furnishes me with only the first part of our mission before we embark.

We know that the only logical reason for us to meet the tanker is that we will be ordered to proceed around the tip of southern Africa. We then expect to navigate through and under the Indian Ocean until we eventually visit our base at Eilat on the Red Sea. Even after the peace treaty, Egypt does not allow our submarines to transit the Suez Canal. So for our submarines to transit from the Mediterranean to the Red Sea, we must take the route all sailors were forced to endure before the canal opened to traffic in 1869. Our orders don't inform us whether we will simply take aboard fuel and supplies in Eilat or make a lengthier visit. The crew knows not to ask any questions. If I'm asked, I simply respond, "Not only don't I know, but I can't tell you if I do know."

CHAPTER 2:
WE'VE GOT ARTISTS

There are many different ways to detect a submarine. One is to listen passively to the sound from the propellers or motors. When we discharge our waste into the ocean or open the outer doors of the torpedo tubes, the sound can sometimes be detected. Passive sonar signifies that there is only listening without the use of the sound "ping" depicted in the movies. The problem with the "ping," or active detection, is that it gives away the presence and location of the device that sends that sound. When active sonar is used, the operator can use the return sound to identify the location and nature of the object that reflects the sound.

There are ways to detect the local disturbance in the earth's magnetic field caused by a submarine's hull. Electric field changes from the submarine's presence can be detected using specialized voltmeters. Sensors can detect the light given off by the ocean's microscopic organisms. This is called bioluminescence. When a submarine passes, the organisms are disturbed, and the level of this disturbance can be measured. If a submarine travels at a high rate of speed near the surface of the ocean, the waves it gives off can be measured, even if they are too small to see with the eye. Changes in water temperature and density at certain depths can give away the presence of a submarine. When a diesel submarine snorkels, it does not merely gulp air. Exhaust gases escape through a second pipe slightly under the surface. The heat of these gases can lead to detection. A pulsed blue-green laser from an aircraft can be used to detect the presence of submarines well below the surface. Even confronted with all these technologies, submarines are difficult to locate, especially in comparison to surface vessels.

One of the main duties of my job is to increase the operational safety of the boat. For this reason and by tradition, I hold private *Dakar* discussions with each member of the crew during the second day of our voyage. *Dakar* is an Israeli submarine that sank during peacetime in January 1968; all sixty-nine sailors aboard perished. At that time, fewer than three million people lived in Israel. So based on proportionate populations, it compares to the loss of six thousand nine hundred American sailors out of an early twenty-first century population of three hundred million. You can imagine the impact of this event. Salvagers raised the bridge and forward edge of her sail in 2000, and they are on display in Haifa. These discussions serve to remind the crewmen of the risk that a moment's inattention can cause for all of us and our families.

I'm sure the Americans and possibly the British, French, or Russians employ the technologies I described to track us at this moment. We now pass through the Strait of Gibraltar. We will not make ourselves easy to hear from a distance. We won't operate our trash disposal system or other noisy equipment. The strait is thirteen kilometers across at its narrowest point. It is at least three hundred meters deep in all areas. Our departure from the Mediterranean for the Atlantic Ocean requires us to fight the current. You see, the evaporation rate in the Mediterranean is larger than the rate of rivers that empty into it. If we choose to fight the current, we will quickly deplete our batteries' charge. We would then increase the risk of detection from the diesels' exhaust gases when we operate them to recharge the batteries. However, if we move slowly, we must spend extra time near the magnetic sensors located in this sensitive transit.

The sailors of our boat maintain certain customs that are designed to boost crew morale. Shortly after we enter the Atlantic Ocean, I initiate our missile-decorating contest. I divide the crew into teams and assign them one of our missiles to "decorate" with marking pens. Everyone participates. My team will always include three men who are among the newest to the boat. For the other teams, I pick combinations of crew that rarely find the opportunity to work together.

Sailors are trained in one of five specialties. The areas of specialization include weapons, navigation, mechanics, electronics, or sonar. In their capacity of missile artists, those with specialized weapons training tend to produce the most colorful artwork. Sailors trained in sonar exhibit the least messy designs. Navigation training usually correlates with the most realistic and detailed portrayal of their subject. If the crew member received mechanical training, expect a creative drawing. Electronics specialists use many lines and favor a largely black color scheme.

The theme of the decorations varies widely. Several are pictures of women, usually with striking but unrealistic shapes. A few exhibit an animal theme; the flying shark is popular. Various "scenic postcards" from the hometown of the crew members take shape. Many take pride in the IDF, the navy, the submarine fleet, or their boat. Several of those show the missiles in use against various imagined targets. Usually these productions include captions directed to the attention of national and terrorist group leaders. An example is "You fool. You think you are the only one with weapons!" They often display precise targeting that allows them to home into the target's rectum before exploding.

I want the three men in my group to take the initiative in the decorating assignment. I ask them to direct me to perform tasks according to their ideas and instructions. I don't need to know their thought process; I want to give them an unforgettable demonstration of the importance of the use of precise language in their orders and reports. They need to be able to tell me, or someone else, that the answer is "no," even if they think the answer I want to hear is "yes." I want them to give me bad news with the same urgency they report good news. They should learn to give suggestions for a course of action or solution to a problem at the same time.

So if the men issue imprecise decoration instructions, I'll deliberately exploit the ambiguity and spoil the decoration. After several inverted mushroom clouds or women with misplaced nipples, they catch on. Even after they learn to give clear-cut instructions, I continue to ruin their designs. This training teaches them that just because they clearly present an oral or written report does not mean the message is received and understood. Once the men are satisfied with my work, I'll covertly blemish their artwork one more time. I'm teaching the men to learn to monitor the work assigned to them. Simply because equipment or a behavior problem appears fixed does not mean it will remain fixed. Inspection is a critical part of our job. Once I make these points of instruction, we get a chance to socialize.

I discover Omri met my mother several years ago. His first year of high school coincided with many bus bombings in Israel. His parents were afraid to have Omri use the buses to travel to school. Omri needed to hitchhike. The high school he attended deservedly held a reputation for academic excellence. Many of the students proudly displayed textbook book covers that featured the name of the school. Others procured book covers from prestigious Israeli universities. Many used book covers obtained from Technion, Israel Institute of Technology, in Haifa. Other students showed off those from Oxford,

Cambridge, or American Ivy League schools. If a family member went to MIT, Stanford, or UCLA, those covers also gave the user status. Omri decided to avoid this competition and to mock it at the same time. He acquired and used book covers from a middle school in a poor neighborhood. So Omri, undersized for his age, decided to hitchhike to school. My mother spots him and picks him up. She observes his book covers and starts to drive him to that school. Omri notices she is not driving the correct route to his school and asks her to take him to the high school. She doesn't believe him, even after he tries to convince her that his books are for the ninth grade. He has to jump out of my mother's car at a stoplight and seek a ride from someone else. So even by age fourteen, Omri learned two lessons. He knows that a person will judge a book by its cover. Of course, he also saw it is impossible to win an argument with my mother.

When the designs are complete, we award prizes. You may have noticed festivals featuring parade floats often include sufficient categories so that each effort receives a ribbon and recognition. Our contest follows this tradition. We also have an overall winner. The overall winners of this round also received recognition for producing the most original design.

The missiles are supplied with various identification markings from the manufacturer and cautions regarding handling, storage, and loading. The navy also adds its own identity numbers and warnings. Most designs either color over these markings or ignore them entirely. The winners of this session's grand prize designed a panel of cartoons that integrated each of these markings into the theme of the cartoon.

The overall theme of the cartoon is a group of men providing advice regarding women to a crewman who is engaged to be married. One panel features a warning against rough handling emerging from the mouth of one cartoon figure. Another man warns of storage of women at extreme temperatures. The next man advises long-term storage must be horizontal. The cautions against saltwater exposure and excessive vibration are also given as advice. The longer serial numbers refer to the number of shoes the woman will likely require and the monthly income required for proper upkeep. The last panel integrates the number three as the punch line of the endeavor with a caution not to trust anything that bleeds for three days and doesn't die.

I also utilize our crew's artistic talents throughout the voyage when we prepare to celebrate each crew member's birthday. The birthday honoree designates crewmen who will participate in the design of his cake. Our crew size generates approximately three birthdays per month. If a crew member's birthday occurred after his last mission with us and before our current mission, we schedule it for a period during which we are not about to celebrate another birthday. Submarine chefs know that items baked in an oven often form uneven shapes due to the maneuvering angles while the item sets. The birthday cakes are an example. Rather than fret about such a possibility, our chefs either purposefully increase the lopsidedness or incorporate it into the cake's design. So our illustrations often include designs that feature the birthday subject holding onto an object on the high side of the cake. When the cake is revealed and sliced, the "high side" slices are the most favored.

Replenishment of fuel and supplies away from our bases is a tricky issue for us. Israel doesn't enjoy good relations with any nations that maintain suitable ports along the Indian Ocean. Almost every government with a port facility in east Africa or Asia falls into one of two categories. Most would rather do us harm than help us. The rest fear the overthrow of their governments if they are shown to provide military assistance to us. So we cannot employ a remote Indian Ocean base.

We have practiced replenishment at sea from a freighter. For the most part, it is not difficult if the seas cooperate. There are several problems, however. First, there is the issue of secrecy. If we use an Israeli ship, then the crew is less likely to directly give away their mission to "interested parties." However, the distance and cost involved combined with the chance these ships are tracked generally rules out their use. The operation risks secrecy without regard to the nationality of the crew operating the ship. We must surface and remain near the freighter while the cargo and fuel is transferred. This required pairing of vessels can tip-off our exact location. Additionally, depending upon the area we rendezvous, the operation may carry a risk of piracy. A large freighter can be a magnet to pirate vessels. The threat to the freighter is greatest immediately before or after the replenishment. If the pirate vessel can detect the presence of the submarine, they know they are outgunned. However, as I say, secrecy is our primary concern.

The accents of the freighter crew we rendezvous with reveal to me that they are South African. The government is no longer friendly toward Israel. However, that nation still has the commercial infrastructure to meet our demands. Their regulation of maritime commerce is spotty and possibly subject to bribery. The government can't enforce any restriction regarding the activity the crew of the ship, which bears a Cape Town registration, now undertakes. I suspect the resources formerly spent to regulate commerce have been diverted to fighting the AIDS epidemic or stemming the tide of refugees from Zimbabwe who seek a better life in South Africa. Our diesel tanks are topped off. We receive powdered milk, powdered eggs, canned meat, and fresh fruit. We now maintain the range to proceed to Eilat.

CHAPTER 3:
SOMEONE NEW

O nce we finish replenishment, we receive the expected instructions ordering us to sail around southern Africa and up the Indian Ocean. The crew welcomes the fresh fruit, although it causes an increase in toilet paper usage. Five days later, we receive our next set of orders. We do not receive the expected instruction to proceed to our naval base in Eilat. We will journey through the Arabian Sea, past the Gulf of Oman, and then past the Strait of Hormuz. We are to enter the Persian Gulf. Our destination is a point that puts even our short-range missiles within range of important Iranian targets. Before we approach the Strait of Hormuz, we are given additional orders.

We receive precise targeting, warhead, and flight-path information for each missile. One is equipped with an antirunway warhead and targets a runway at an air force base. Many are intended for radar installations. Others are directed at antiaircraft missile sites near nuclear facilities. We are given a launch sequence for the missiles.

Two of our Popeye Turbos are to have nuclear "bunker buster" warheads installed. Their flight paths terminate at nuclear research and production facilities. They are not set for launch with the other "package."

The conclusion of the message contains coded information for my eyes only regarding the probability of launch. Drills are designated as such. If there should be an emergency, I know whether to interrupt the programming and loading activity to focus our attention on an injured crewman, for example. Our crew programs and installs all varieties of conventional and nuclear warheads on every mission. I've always known our activities amounted to realistic training, even if the crew did not. This time, the orders pertaining to the conventional warheads inform me that the probability of launch is high. I am to make contact when I reach the launch point for final confirmation of whether to launch. The probability of launch of the nuclear-tipped missiles is designated under the classification "moderate." We must receive authorization containing prearming codes before we would launch them.

From the time Iran embarked on its nuclear program, all responses in opposition to that program fell into three variations. The first option would be to apply pressure against the government to reverse course by applying increasingly harsh economic and diplomatic sanctions. The second option would be for a military attack to at least delay the program. The third option would be to accept a nuclear-armed Iran. When the American intelligence report citing the probable suspension of Iranian weapons development reached the world community, it eliminated the consensus required for the world to impose effective sanctions. It also undermined support for an American military attack. For Israel, having a nuclear-armed Iran is not an option. Iran has funded and supplied terrorist proxies on Israel's borders in recent years. Even if it never detonated a nuclear weapon, mere possession of such a device would give that government carte blanche to dictate policies to other nations and use increasingly deadly tactics against opponents. So with only the military option available, the receipt of the targeting package I told you about seemed inevitable.

I allow myself several moments to speculate in regard to the complete attack plan. Although our launch would give away our position, comparatively speaking, we remained relatively safe from attack by the Iranians. The air crews and any ground forces assigned to the mission faced extreme danger. Who among those forces would be killed, or worse, captured? The attack against the Iraqi nuclear plant in 1981, along with the later overthrow of the Iraqi government, brought an end of the nuclear threat from that country for decades. The attack against the Syrian nuclear plant in 2007, like the one against the Iraqi facility, struck a building that did not yet house a fueled reactor. Both operations were confined to a single facility.

Iran has dispersed its facilities over wide areas. Some are situated deep underground, but others are placed near populated areas. Several of the sites, including their reactor, contain nuclear materials. The architects of the Iranian nuclear program ensured that their facilities could not be destroyed easily. The presence of the involuntary human shields who worked and lived nearby would serve to further deter an attack against the facilities.

I don't have time now to focus upon these considerations. We will shortly enter one of the most patrolled and economically important shipping areas on the planet. It is also a body of water with an average depth of only fifty meters and a maximum depth of barely ninety meters.

In deep water, we can often deploy our towed array sonar—basically a long cable with hydrophones attached to the end. It provides us longer-range listening capability and minimizes the "deaf" spot to our rear caused by the hull-mounted sonar's limitations. But we cannot deploy the device here. The shallow depth of the water in the Gulf risks snagging the towed array against the seafloor or objects, including shipwrecks that protrude from the bottom. Also, our frequent course changes would reduce the effectiveness of the array. So our listening capabilities will have to suffer with a deaf spot. But so will other submarines.

As we enter the Strait of Hormuz, I plan to find an empty tanker to follow, so that her noise and the magnetic image from her hull can mask our own presence. I can't follow the first one because sonar reveals she already has an American attack submarine following her. This discovery removes all doubt of whether an American task force operates within or is about to enter the Gulf. The next tanker is even larger and noisier than the last one. Its destination is likely a port north of our destination. We pull beneath and behind it. Our sonarmen are busy. They must hear and interpret subtle changes in sound that enable us to maintain the proper distance from the tanker. At the same time, they must listen for the sounds that indicate we are tracked or have been discovered.

We arrive on station, a several square kilometer area specified within our orders. Headquarters knows we won't be able to extend our underwater antenna. We must ascend to a depth that permits us to extend our communications mast to the surface. I strive not to operate at a shallow depth in such a highly patrolled section of the Gulf because of the increased risk of detection. However, it is necessary to receive the signal from the navy. The signal we receive from our navy is clear. It is the repeating "standby" signal. While we wait, we start our diesels to recharge our batteries.

We've now remained on station for an hour. When we conduct drills, headquarters usually orders us to cancel the launch alert shortly after we reach our destination. After another hour on station, the sonar operators' hydrophones detect the sound of a helicopter; later, they pick up the sound of sonobuoys entering the water near us. Submarine hunting forces are looking for us and accomplishing their goal. We can't submerge deeper or we lose communications. So we cannot take any action to avoid this contact. After what seems like a day but is just under three hours on the clock, we finally receive a message that withdraws the possibility of launch and orders our exit from the Persian Gulf.

We leave the Gulf under the watch of aircraft or helicopters that drop additional sonobuoys. It is always unsettling to have our boat's stealth compromised, even during training. I can't help sweating our detection, even though I suspect only the Americans maintain the capability to track us this well. The emotional side of my brain is only slightly comforted knowing our American friends maintain such an excellent submarine-tracking capability.

We all expect to receive orders to allow us to proceed to Eilat. Instead, we are directed to journey to the large Indian naval base at Mumbai. I presume our headquarters wants to minimize our risk of detection in port. Eilat has no submarine pens. The presence of a submarine at the docks would be impossible for a spy satellite to miss. There are other lower-technology ways to confirm our presence at the base, which lies a slight distance from Jordan and not far from Saudi and Egyptian territory. If we don't make port in Eilat, our adversaries must assume we remain on patrol. If we are on patrol, they must presume their nation is within range of our missiles.

There is an additional order. It takes the form of a standardized letter. I'll tell you what it says:

Stationing of Noncrew Personnel Aboard Your Vessel:

Upon arrival at the previously designated port, you will board and house aboard your vessel, until further notice, the officer identified below. The ununiformed officer will arrive at the security perimeter of your vessel at the top of the second hour after your arrival in port. You are to personally identify and escort the officer to your vessel. You are then to inspect and search the officer's baggage and person per standard procedures concerning admitting personnel aboard a vessel outside a secure base. The officer's duties and expertise will be provided for your ears only. The officer is subject to your command and discipline concerning matters affecting the operation of your vessel. You are ordered to facilitate the advancement and completion of the officer's assignment including additional assignments, if any, designated by the officer's unit commander.

Name of officer: Sharon Ben-Zinger
Unit: Mamtam
Identification information: Valid Identification Card
(confirm hologram)

Signed,
Deputy Commander, Navy

* * *

Mamtam is a small unit based at Haifa. Their unit symbol is an owl. Their members include the computer nerds responsible for all communications and computer infrastructure for the Israeli navy. They have served occasional short missions aboard submarines. It is unusual for one to board during a visit to a foreign port.

We follow other orders to help mask our identity while in port. We surface near the Indian naval base. Binyamin has drawn the duty of applying heavy grease to obscure our identification markings. I suspect he earned this dirty assignment from his chief as a remedy for Binyamin's overconcern for his cleanliness. Of course, this form of therapy only ensures an endless cycle between extremes of filth and cleanliness.

When we arrive at the port, we are under orders to have the crew remain on the boat and not engage in any behavior that might lead observers to believe we are anything other than an Indian navy submarine. So unlike our visits to an Israeli port, we will not be able to catch up with news from our families and friends. Most of us will not set foot off the boat.

Our approach to the harbor reveals antiaircraft weapons deployed on the hills overlooking the harbor. The base maintains a large complement of soldiers and numerous military vehicles. We come on deck only a few men at a time, and we wear raincoats to cover our uniforms when we are up top.

Diesel fuel is pumped into our tanks until they are full, and we take delivery of sealed containers filled with the special motor oil we need for our diesels. We receive a welcome take-out order. Our contact purchased eighty orders of curry chicken from a local restaurant. It is an unusual treat for us to consume freshly cooked meat. The fresh food we take on board at the beginning of the mission is prized but doesn't last long. We carry little food that requires refrigeration. A large size refrigeration unit would consume too much precious battery power and occupy too much prized space.

We also receive a package of kitchen spices and condiments, toilet paper, and other consumables. The food we receive includes lots of uncooked rice, powdered eggs and milk, canned fish, and a large supply of Indian military "just add water" meals. I'm a bit disappointed we will not receive fruit or vegetables other than bananas. Apparently, headquarters does not trust Indian sanitation procedures. For some reason, we also receive ten Indian cinema DVDs with semipornographic covers. I'll add them to our library later.

The alarm on my watch reminds me that I must meet the intelligence officer. One hour and twenty-five minutes after our arrival, I step onto the dock to meet him. I had informed the crew only that we will take on an additional Mamtam officer and that I'll share what I'm allowed to divulge after I interview him.

So I attempt to locate Mr. Ben-Zinger and my "land legs" simultaneously. I notice a woman leave the side of a man and make her way to the security perimeter struggling to carry a large duffel bag. I think Mr. Ben-Zinger makes a poor impression if he can't carry his own provisions and uses a woman to hand them off to me. The woman asks me if I need to check her identification. I don't understand what her point is and tell her so, but she insists. At that point, I comprehend I have just met Sharon Ben-Zinger. I wonder whether headquarters did not provide this information in order to be politically correct. Perhaps they were only incompetent.

Sharon is a name that can be either male or female. It is pronounced identically to the last name of Israel's former prime minister. I simply assumed the officer would be a man. I start to offer to carry her bag but then think the better of it, so I let her struggle to the gangway.

You have to remember the men haven't seen a woman since the Dead Sea was alive. They are at a complete loss to process what their eyes feed their brain. If they knew in advance that a female would not merely pass close to them but would share their boat, I'm sure they would have stood upright with their chests out instead of frozen in place with their mouths open.

She looks relieved to wrestle the duffel across the gangplank. She doesn't realize the bag still must be lowered through the hatch and down the ninety-degree ladder before it can be taken aboard. I didn't want any injuries on my boat, so I lower the bag through the hatch to Yonatan. She climbs down, employing small, deliberate steps. I lead her to my cabin. I barely stop myself from apologizing to her for the door thresholds, low ceilings, and smells emanating from the boat.

By the time we arrive at my cabin, I have my plan. I will inspect her belongings and interview her regarding her duties at the same time. In the process, I hope to discover any incorrect assumptions she brought aboard and correct them. I want to determine whether she could handle confinement in the boat and, at minimum, not create any emergencies.

I ask once again for her identification and this time do

a better job at matching the picture with the face. I check the hologram and read her title that says simply "intelligence officer." I notice she will celebrate her birthday in only a few days. I will have to exercise caution while selecting the crewmen I assign to design her cake.

I will not pat her down. I will confirm that she does not carry contraband or devices planted on her person or baggage aboard the boat. I convert myself into a cross between an airport screener and the booking officer at a jail. I first confirm that she packed her own bag. I verify it remained under her control. I confirm that no one asked her to carry anything for them and that no strangers "bumped" her. I ask her if she has anything that could be considered contraband or dangerous to carry on a submarine. I'm about to give her examples.

Before I can, she pulls out a piece of paper and reads "flammable or combustible materials? No, I thought your torpedo room has enough," she adds.

She tells me she left her toxic materials in her ex-boyfriend's house.

"Corrosive materials? Is the acid in the boat's batteries becoming too weak?"

She continues this response with each item on the list: oxidizing materials, aerosol containers, compressed gases, ammunition, weapons, explosives, explosive actuated devices, propellants, pyrotechnics, chemical and biological warfare material, medical waste, infectious materials, and radioactive materials, pointing out where the submarine already employs these items. I'm amused, but I don't think the safety of the boat and everyone aboard can be risked for purposes of amusement. She observes that I'm not smiling and then informs me she carries pharmaceutical supplies in the duffel.

Don't misunderstand me. I understand humor is a sign of intelligence and a good way to calm one's nerves. I merely believe my participation in a ballet of wits in the midst of a safety discussion would send the wrong message. I educate her concerning the difference between the systems that give us breathable air and the dangerous oxidizing materials we carry, but she must not bring aboard the boat.

Before I have her reveal what she has brought on board inside the duffel, I direct her to empty her pockets. The pockets are already empty except for the foil and plastic bubble from a seasickness pill. Her pants cuffs are clean, and there is nothing attached to the bottom of her shoes.

I ask her to show me the contents of the duffel and explain how it accomplishes the mission. She shows me her naval intelligence officer's uniform. She doesn't need to explain this item to me. She tells me it is to remind the crew that she is an officer and to remind herself that she is on an assignment. While she neatly stacks her undergarments on the uniform, we both miss any opportunity to joke. She then removes a large laptop computer. Only after she stacks several large auxiliary hard drives on top does she give me any information. She informs me she is here to supplement our intelligence and strategic deterrence capabilities.

"Particularly in regard to attack of distant targets," she adds nonchalantly.

I ask her to describe the contents of the hard drives. She tells me they hold commercial and military satellite images of the areas her superiors deem relevant to the mission. She also gives me a flash drive that contains updated information concerning deployments of allied, neutral, and hostile armed forces. She displays several other flash drives.

"They contain the most sensitive information because they are easier to destroy," she explains.

"Here are the pharmaceuticals," she announces.

She shows me a large quantity and assortment of sea sickness remedies and some acetaminophen. She has earplugs and a sleep mask.

Then she shows me some tampons and pads and shows

off her knowledge, "I know—used ones in the trash, not the toilet."

She unpacks her reading material. A several hundred page spiral bound group of papers with a cover titled "The Search for Spiders" appears. She shows me it is really the Mamtam book that explains techniques that can be used to hack military and other secured Web sites. Lastly, she displays a paperback romance novel and today's *Mumbai Mirror* newspaper. I consider taking away the romance novel, but I know better than to take away a crewman's "security item." Besides, she should find herself too busy to read it. I give her two instructions. First, she needs to remove or hide the cover of the novel so that the men don't get the wrong idea. Second, I tell her not to throw away the newspaper. It can be our backup toilet paper. However, because we treat it as semicombustible, it must be stored in an enclosed area.

She surrenders the paper to me and declares, "Here you go. I've already read it."

She tells me, "Thank you for your concern," and then tears off the cover of the novel and gives it to me.

Her statements and behavior enable me to draw several conclusions about her. She will respect my authority and will not create conflict over unimportant issues. She understands she should not fuel any sexual aggression by the men. She has almost certainly lied regarding the newspaper, which appeared unopened. I don't consider her statement to me to signify her dishonesty; I consider it a reflection of her prioritization. I'm impressed that when she saw that I treated this meeting seriously, she toned down her jokes. I'm sure she suppressed repeating some gag that mentions the use of sunscreen or screen doors.

I tell her that I'll have someone secure her computer and the hard drives so they are not damaged during the boat's maneuvers once we determine a suitable location for her workstation. Then I turn to a serious safety issue. I ask her to describe her experience with submarines. She tells me she took part in a tour of *Dolphin* shortly after that submarine appeared at Israel's sixtieth birthday celebration. What I tell her is harsh but necessary. I tell her to devote all her waking hours not spent on her intelligence assignment to studying a manual I'm about to give her. It is a basic review of the submarine, its layout, safety procedures, and restrictions.

I caution Sharon that while use of the toilet is an event whose sound cannot be heard by those attempting to track us, the discharge of the waste from the toilet into the ocean can be heard. It is not permitted when we need to remain quiet. If the tanks are full and must be discharged, the operation involves opening and closing valves in a precise sequence and under specific conditions. I will have her practice with a crew member while we are in port. I will then test her. She also has to know where to proceed during emergencies and emergency drills. She must be trained to perform emergency escape procedures. But she can't practice the procedures to gain the level of proficiency the rest of the crew has attained.

Most of the officers and men remain too busy to train her. There is another consideration. I need someone who will respect her in her official rank. They must not grow distracted either by her or by the others who will stare at them. I need someone who can complete the job in a professional manner.

Yigal is probably the last man you would want on your team during a physically challenging activity. He is thin and awkward for a submariner. He knows the boat's systems better than most of his mates with twice the experience but lacks confidence in his own abilities. So I summon Yigal and instruct him to give Sharon a quick tour, highlighting safety issues. I inform him I expect his task to last at least an hour, and I order him to report to me immediately upon its completion.

If I tell you not to think of pink elephants, what do you think of? You see, our crew faces a similar paradox. I've got to inform our crew that they must ignore her and focus on their work. I must caution them against both hazing and overly friendly behavior. However, I can't empower Sharon to ruin the career of a man who behaves no worse to her than they would to another crewman. I don't want to turn behavior of the type she used to ignore on dry land into something offensive because of where she now lives and works.

I must make arrangements for her bunk. Before I knew I would be assigned a female to house, I planned to use a semi-hot-bunking arrangement with one of the junior officers. A male intelligence officer would have shared the bunk of an officer who maintained a different sleep schedule. I have to rethink my plan. The other officers sleep in slightly less cramped bunks than the enlisted men but within a common small compartment. I don't want to lose my command over any of the ways this arrangement could offend her. She might hear one of the men taking care of business with a crusty sock. She might even find the one used by the man whose bunk she occupied. I also don't want to distract the men in the room. They need to forget she is aboard this boat. They can't concern themselves with competition for her attention or approval.

I also don't want to put her through conditions where she might turn claustrophobic. The world is full of excellent sailors who can't handle submarine duty. She is not even a sailor. So I can't bunk her in one of the pull-down racks we utilize for special operations forces. The only logical place for her to bunk is my cabin. It won't be much of a hardship for me. I'm rarely there more than six hours a day.

I also must find a place for her workstation. The existing communications area is already crowded. Even if I can rework the area to add an additional workstation, I'm sure her presence would distract the men. However, if she needs her computer to connect to our communications antenna and printers, the submarine has no other locations that meet her requirements. I need to find out more concerning the nature of her assignment aboard *Tekumah*.

Before long, Yigal returns. He doesn't say anything, but I

can easily interpret his expression. His smile says, "Thanks for selecting me for this assignment. I owe you one." I quiz her regarding the location of safety equipment and the location of the boat's compartments. I should have her climb up the hatch she stepped down a few hours ago. However, I don't want her to think I am putting her in a position that enables us to stare at her rear while she concentrates on hand and foot holds. I also don't want her to practice this type of climb if it might trigger claustrophobia.

I dismiss Yigal. I ask Sharon if she has any questions. She wants to know where her workstation will be located. I ask her to advise me whether her computer must access the communications system and printers on the boat. She informs me she does not require such access since she can transfer data between the computers by means of the portable hard drives. She expects to make use of the boat's communications stations that use the Internet and radio. But she realizes these services will be available infrequently. She knows we could only employ these forms of communications when we operate at a sufficiently shallow depth.

"Also under conditions where doing so does not risk detection," I add.

I tell her that I'll locate her equipment in my cabin. While she is there, she can keep an eye on the depth gauge or listen for intercom messages that will reveal to her if we are at a depth that enables communication. There is a moment of silence while she thinks of her response. Then the questions come out like bullets from an Uzi.

"What will the crew think? How will you work or sleep if I'm in your room? Would you do this if I were a man?"

I tell her the crew will understand, but if they don't, they will accept the situation. I let her know that I rarely perform any work within my cabin. I'm all over the boat. I tell her that if I need to sleep, I'll gently evict her. However, if her work is at a critical point, I'll find another bunk.

"I'm the commander. They're all my bunks," I add.

I'm a little harsh with my response to the last question. I'm not used to having my orders questioned.

"Of course, I wouldn't put you here if you were a man. I wouldn't need to. The potential for inappropriate interactions between you and the crew requires your workstation be separate from the crew."

I hope I've stated the obvious. She appears to understand, if not accept, my point.

She wants to know where she will be able to bunk "without inappropriate interactions," borrowing my phrase.

"For the same reasons I told you a moment ago, you will bunk in my cabin when I'm not there. We'll post a sign on the door that indicates you are either working or sleeping there."

Now she is concerned the men will not respect her and think I've played favorites. She reminds me about the women who serve in the capacity of combat pilots in the IDF. She tells me that a Norwegian navy submarine once employed a female submarine commander.

I have two choices for my response. I can remind her that I'm giving a lawful order she is bound to follow and save time. Instead, I realize the importance of convincing her.

I remind her that combat pilots are one- or two-person crews and that their missions last merely a few hours. The Norwegian female submarine commander undoubtedly completed submarine training and endured years of service on submarines or other vessels. I smile, imagining a Norwegian woman wrestling a large submersible pump while a compartment fills with high pressure water. Sharon did not undergo submarine training. I remind her she is not part of the crew but merely attached to my command.

I don't think my answer completely satisfies her, but she knows not to persist. I make arrangements to secure the computer to my desk and the hard drives to the floor.

CHAPTER 4:
CAN YOU CONNECT THE DOTS?

We turn around quickly and leave about forty-five minutes before dawn. After we exit the harbor and perform our trim dive, I make a mistake. I forget to translate for Sharon what I mean when I order "up and down bubbles." You might think I'm perpetrating the hazing that I otherwise forbid aboard the boat. This is not true. I am not a tour guide. Anyway, Sharon's upset stomach exceeded the design limits of the seasickness pill. Fortunately, she cleaned up after herself. Regrettably, when she threw away her dirty rag, she only thought she disposed of it in the trash. She tossed the smelly rag in the container used for exchange or "reading" material. So those of us who looked forward to our time with "Sexy Nurses" will have to put up with "Sexy Nurses Who Smell of Vomited Curry."

Our new orders require us to patrol in the area midway between Oman and India. I brief the crew and also give my talk concerning Sharon. I explain her work location and the split sleep arrangements. I emphasize that she should not be interrupted in her work. The crew should not inquire regarding the nature of her duties. Further, they should make only necessary comments about her. However, they should respond to every appropriate request for assistance. Anyone who inappropriately touches her, makes comments to her, or glances at her in a hostile or lurid way will be reported. If I am the perpetrator, the report should be made to the executive officer. Naftali will then communicate the report to headquarters at the earliest opportunity. Otherwise, I should personally receive all other reports of violations. I end with the order that if a crewman can't work under these conditions, he is to report to me.

On our way out of the harbor, we receive commercial broadcast news. Israel and the Palestinians have agreed to the broad terms of a peace agreement. Only a few details remain for negotiations. The news describes the terms. The Palestinians receive 96 percent of the West Bank, a share of Jerusalem, and a large number of refugees are allowed to "return" to live with relatives inside Israel. Other Arab refugees from 1948 and their descendants are to receive large compensation. Almost every Palestinian prisoner will be released over a period of months, and the new Palestinian state will maintain its own autonomous borders and airfields. In return, Israel receives promises of eventual normalization of relations with most of the Arab world and a promise to settle remaining territorial claims without use of force.

The terms of the agreement cause distress among many of our crew. I have to remind them to put the news behind them and concentrate on our duties. I can do little to lift their spirits but remind them that implementation of the agreement will take time and Knesset approval, and there will be plenty of time to digest the news when more details become available.

I depend upon the senior enlisted member of the crew, Rami, to keep the enlisted men focused on their duties. He is nicknamed "Rambo," only because of his name rather than his physique. We serve four meals within each twenty-four hour period. Rami rarely misses one of them. He uses this time to get to know the men on a personal level. He stands up for his men when he speaks to me. Of equal importance, he explains my position to the enlisted men. He knows how to lead people to perform their assignment rather than push them. The officers realize that while they outrank Rami, he knows more in regard to the boat's systems and has received many more promotions than they have. I remind Rami to find something praiseworthy regarding each man every day and to give the praise publicly. Rami performs well at attacking problems, not people. In this regard, he outperforms several of our junior officers.

We head out into the Indian Ocean. The next time we ascend to snorkeling depth, we hear more astonishing news. An American guided missile destroyer detonated an Iranian mine in the Persian Gulf. The ship is heavily damaged, and there is substantial loss of life.

For you conspiracy theorists, our boat operated well out of range of this portion of the Persian Gulf. While I can't inform you of the whereabouts of the other Israeli *Dolphin*-class submarines or our surface ships and aircraft during this incident, you should be satisfied that Iran deliberately deployed mines for the purpose of inflicting harm on the Americans. In fact, the Iranian news services touted the "sinking" of a "trespassing" American ship—that is, for the few hours until they were taken off the air during the American counterstrike.

As we already suspected, the Americans had positioned several aircraft carrier battle groups within or just outside the Persian Gulf. These forces, combined with those based within Iraq, Diego Garcia, and even the United States, hit back at the Iranian naval facilities. They also struck airfields, missile bases, "regime targets," and the known nuclear weapons development facilities.

We all hope we will receive orders to return either to Eilat or Haifa. We've already served a long mission. There is no update to our previous orders.

Our next round of operations at communication depth

brings more broadcast news. We learn of the overthrow of the unstable post-Musharraf Pakistani government. Apparently, the radical Islamists persuaded the Pakistani military not to confront the demonstrators who believed either that Pakistan should help Iran or that their government had aligned itself too closely with the Americans. The previous government fled for a safe haven and was replaced by a new government composed of radical Islamists. Pakistan is far enough away from Israel that usually I wouldn't concern myself with this type of news. However, Pakistan is a nuclear power. If you add that power to the belief that all Hindus, Christians, Jews, and nonradicalized Muslims must be converted or destroyed, you have many megatons of reasons to worry.

We hope the Americans will continue to degrade the ability of Iran to make war. I also hope they can cause a countercoup or otherwise reduce the danger from the events in Pakistan.

Our updated orders arrive. I bear the burden of reporting our assignment to our still-disappointed crew. We are ordered to patrol near the Pakistani port of Gwadar. We will observe and report unusual commercial activities—for example, transfer of cargo between ships. I expect our contact reports will be forwarded to either the American or the Indian armed forces.

Sharon has provided me with more details concerning her work. Her duties involve the upgrade of the targeting system of both types of missiles we carry. The satellite and aerial photos, if sufficiently up-to-date, can be used to increase the accuracy of the missiles. It can also be critical if the missiles can't access and process GPS information. I imagine her hard drives contain images of every potential military target and defensive system of our enemies and any unstable neutral nations.

For someone who shares my cabin, I don't encounter Sharon much, which is fine. I have advanced her duties during emergency drills. I assign her progressively more difficult safety tasks to enhance her self-esteem. She can put on a fire-resistant suit, pull the release pin on a fire extinguisher, and pretend to sweep the base of imaginary fires. If there is a real fire, the men will fight it while she samples and reports the quality of the atmosphere in the compartments farthest away from the fire.

I have a stereotypical image of a female in a traditionally male environment. Usually, they are so unattractive that they realize their looks can't attract a man with sufficient earning power to provide for them. They comprehend they will have to make a good living through their own efforts and choose a profession for that reason. Sharon does not fit this mold. Another possibility is the woman will take serious measures to complete the required education and training or perform the work, but simply wants to exploit the opportunity to mingle with professional men in order to select one to target. Sharon appears to work diligently without the need to impress anyone, so she does not validate my assumption in this regard.

A submarine is a poor environment for many things. Staying dry is the best example. However, it is the perfect environment for rumors. The crew of *Tekumah* has many theories concerning Sharon.

One line of thought is that she is part of an evil conspiracy that involves the American government's efforts to rein in the Israeli military. The timing of Sharon's placement aboard *Tekumah* adds fuel to this line of speculation. The theory also receives support from the past few weeks' events. Supposedly, the Americans uncovered the order for our imminent attack against Iran while we navigated toward our launch point in the Persian Gulf. The crew knows that we loaded antirunway warheads aboard our missiles. They deduce we were assigned the air defense suppression portion of a mission to attack Iran by air. The theory suggests an American order to our command to cancel our attack. To ensure the order was followed, the Americans tracked us when we left the Persian Gulf. They forced Israel to agree to a settlement with the Palestinians. In return, the Americans launched a more damaging strike against

Iran than Israel could have unleashed. The scheme considers Sharon's presence aboard *Tekumah* to fulfill an important additional American requirement. Allegedly, working from my cabin, she would change critical computer programs to eliminate our nuclear capability.

The other line of speculation considers that Sharon is all-powerful. A number of the men think she carries updated attack plans, even launch codes. In this way, we would not need to communicate with headquarters. A variation of this theory suggests her computer programs can defeat certain forms of antisubmarine warfare, making us more undetectable.

Another rumor envisages her presence to constitute a test regarding the presence of females aboard submarines. The followers of this idea ignore her failure to attend submarine school. This theory also disregards the long-standing policy of the navy that before an important change can be made to an operational submarine, the theory must prove successful within a training environment.

I've even learned that several of the men believe headquarters wants her to seduce me to force me out of my command. The previous executive officer supposedly orchestrated this plot in order to gain his revenge against me for having sought his replacement.

If the men have an impression that I'm happy regarding her assignment to the boat, I don't hear about it.

The unflattering speculation regarding Sharon's presence does not inhibit the men from changing their bathing habits. Not one of the men fails to take advantage of his allotted shower day. This change does not cause a problem. However, the average time in the shower and water usage increases to unacceptable levels. I remind the men of the definition of a submarine shower. There are also more accidents "requiring" a crewman to wash irritating chemicals from his body.

Boris's elastic weight-training bands are in heavy demand.

I'm sure he is owed a few favors for lending their use. Hair and beards are now trimmed and combed regularly for the first time.

Sharon's turn in the shower requires special procedures, but we manage. She eats in the compartment that converts into the officer's mess during mealtimes. I think the officers have started to slow their eating a little since she has shared their mess with them. They still eat faster than she does, but they now understand they should not leave until they all finish eating. I know headquarters is not interested whether the presence of a female will civilize us, but it has some effect.

I must develop another special procedure because of Sharon. Her birthday cake will be created under parameters that I determine. First, she does not know the men on the crew well enough to select who should create her cake. More importantly, I can't risk the chance they might create an offensive design that distracts her from her duties or even causes her to complain. I pick three men to design her cake. They must show me a detailed drawing of their design for my approval.

The first two proposals validate my decision to monitor the design. The first sketch features Sharon in the torpedo room polishing a torpedo with my name on it. Most likely, the designers merely wanted to use the opportunity of their appointment to tease me concerning their imagination of my relationship with her. They can't have expected I would approve such a design. The second design envisions Sharon dressed in a short skirt, reaching up while she strings laundry on a clothesline that runs down from the submarine's extended periscope. Despite the men's assurance that my name will not appear on the underwear she is pinning, I've got to disapprove this design. Not only does the design emphasize Sharon's idealized figure, but it depicts her performing domestic duties. I expect she might be able to handle this level of teasing, but I don't want to stake my career on the design of a birthday cake. So this sketch of "Sharon the laundress" joins the one of "Sharon the torpedo polisher" in my cabin's trash. Ultimately, after threatening to hand the assignment over to another committee, I see a design I can allow. Her cake will feature the owl that symbolizes her intelligence unit caught in our submarine's propeller.

The birthday observance proceeds well. She rewards the designers with slices from the "high side," which in this case turned out to be a high corner. She reserves the owl for herself and the propeller for me.

We spend approximately one week observing and remaining unobserved. It is difficult to know if what we are observing is normal for these waters. We are probably the first Israeli vessel to patrol this area for an extended time. Most of the traffic involves container ships with registered destinations to Japan or China. We don't spot any traffic that is heading from Pakistan to the Persian Gulf except several small oil tankers. We keep watch on a small part of a large Pakistani coast. None of us has any illusions that we enjoy more than the slightest chance of stumbling across activity that would trigger the need to make a report, much less engage in hostilities.

Tekumah is about to enter an area full of mines.

You see, I have a few problems with Sharon's conduct. I've warned her, but she sometimes leaves her computer unfastened to my desk. If we must employ a violent maneuver, it might be damaged. Also, I think she uses the computer to play games excessively rather than work. Of course, everyone needs free time. Her mission is of such importance that we had to take her aboard during the middle of the mission. She should apply more of her day to her work.

I'm not sure how to handle the problem. I don't want to give her more leeway than the crewmen for violation of rules. On the other hand, I am the only one who knows what she does. If I discipline her and she gets upset, then there will be talk of a "lover's quarrel." I can't have that. She could even complain about me when we arrive back at Haifa. I know many men who have had their careers tarnished due to unjustified complaints by women.

Even without regard to any actions taken by women, they can influence men to make poor choices. I don't want to make one here.

I told you before that my brother died in Lebanon. I did not give you the whole story. He served Israel in the capacity of an officer of an elite infantry brigade. He earned a promotion for his efforts to improve relations with villagers in southern Lebanon. The promotion included the right to return to his unit's Israeli base to instruct other infantry officers who were about to be deployed to Lebanon. He received a letter from his girlfriend stating she did not want to see him anymore. He felt upset and humiliated by the news. His feelings played a large part in his decision to turn down the new assignment in order to remain in Lebanon with his unit. He died in an ambush three weeks to the day after he received the letter from his girlfriend.

I told you my other sibling died in a car crash. She was my sister—the baby of the family. She was a passenger in a car driven by her boyfriend. He drove recklessly in an effort to impress her and crashed into a parked car, killing her. I don't have to tell you the effect this event had upon our family.

I'm sure these experiences have clouded my relationships with women. Most seem to have interest only in confusing my judgment sufficiently to have me spend money and attention on them until someone wealthier or more prestigious comes along. Many show minimal evidence that they are people of substance. If I push the right buttons, they are happy with their lives; they maintain no interest in events outside their own world. They don't have any set of principles, and they don't care to learn about my values.

I decide a course of action concerning Sharon and her game playing. I'll steer a middle course between two minefields. I'll continue to warn her that she has to keep the game playing to a minimum and prod her regarding her progress concerning the targeting work. The unfastened computer will be permanently attached to the floor if she cannot secure it consistently.

CHAPTER 5:
YOU REMEMBER WHAT YOU WERE DOING?

$\mathbf{E}$vents of this nature always are such that you remember where you were and what you were doing. I expect you remember where you were too. I'm reviewing the tests of the specific gravity of our batteries. One of the special officers, Danny, knocks on my cabin door. I can't even start to say "shalom" before his mouth starts to quiver. No words form. He takes me to the radio communications headphones. He still quivers while I adjust the headphones. I listen to a broadcast news reporter interviewing people in Beirut, Lebanon. They tell the network anchor that people remain panicked regarding the two flashes of light from the direction of Israel. The anchor then recaps that most of Israel and western Jordan has been cut off from communications with the rest of the world. They are unable to reach their correspondents in Tel Aviv, Jerusalem, the West Bank, or Amman, Jordan. They offer no reason for the flashes and communications failure.

Danny then switches me to an internet news report with essentially the same news. The banner at the bottom of the screen gives the approximate time of the flashes and adds the ominous words "mushroom cloud." I have the impression he shows me this level of corroboration to convince me he is not engaging in deceptive behavior. I ask him which other crew members know this information, and he tells me that we are the only two so far.

I call a meeting with the special officers and my executive officer in the torpedo/missile room. I choose this room for several reasons. That location is one area large enough for all of us to meet, and it is located at one end of the boat; it is not used as a passageway. We have met there before when other compartments were not available. It will not be alarming when I ask the crew members to take a break for a while. I want my executive officer, Naftali, to join Danny and the other three officers. Procedurally, I need to inform him of this news since he serves in the role of my backup. Also, he can add his opinion regarding the subject of how their receipt of this news might affect crew performance. Procedures require me to include the other three special officers: Yossi, Sergei, and Noam. Plus, I want to give them the news in a more calming way than Danny.

My duty includes the task of giving death notifications. Unfortunately, I am experienced in this regard. This task is not in the same category. I explain that we have news reports with confirmation only by other news reports. We do not know the cause of this event. We do not possess a damage assessment, and we do not have a party to blame. We also maintain comfort in that we enjoy at least thirty days worth of fuel and food. I ask Naftali if he recommends we keep the news from the crew until we know more. We know the advantage a better-rested crew provides. We may need to call upon them to toil longer hours under tough conditions later. He does not think the loss of trust from the delay will outweigh this advantage. We agree that our secrecy will be temporary. When we have new orders or details concerning the cause or extent of the attack from an official source, "we all go to war together." We would inform the crew.

We will spend more time over the next day at a depth permitting us to receive communications. The special officers listen for orders from our naval headquarters. Although our receiver works perfectly, this frequency remains silent. The officers also establish a schedule to monitor the broadcast news. Following procedures, we also start to check the "emergency order" Internet mailboxes.

For the next several hours, there is not much change in the news reports. Our naval headquarters' frequency remains mute. Finally, the American president makes a statement. We record it from the radio. He wants all Americans to pray for the safety of those affected by the unknown event. He urges the world not to jump to conclusions. Intelligence agencies are analyzing satellite data in order to assess the cause and extent of damage. Also, American aircraft will deploy to survey the area. Naval forces already in the Mediterranean, along with European and Iraqi-based aircraft, will assist in the investigation. Disaster assistance teams are alerted and prepared to move. He gives out a series of phone numbers. He recites one number for people to call with information or questions concerning Americans feared to be located within the affected area. There is another number for disaster assistance pledges. No specific threat against the United States has been announced or detected. American military forces and civilian specialists would, however, redouble their efforts to detect and thwart any attack planned against the United States.

I hold another meeting with the same group of men. Yossi wants to know if we shouldn't head up the Red Sea to our base at Eilat. He expects we will soon receive orders to assess the damage directly or join the fight. At minimum, we can use our generators to provide electricity and our distillers to provide clean water. Even before I could answer, the others remind him that our orders require a different course of action. Since we still do not have more definite information or new orders, we will continue to keep our secret and hope the crew does not turn suspicious of our behavior. After a while, they are sure to notice our meetings, obsession with the radio, and change in disposition. I tell the special officers that I'll inform Sharon and swear her to secrecy as well.

Sharon has apparently slept or worked without the need to approach the communications area. She emerges from my quarters to use the toilet. I ask her to see me when she is done. When Sharon finds me, she wears an expression on her face that suggests I've caught her doing something wrong. I have so far avoided us spending time together in my cabin to avoid any appearance of impropriety. I certainly don't want the crew to observe Sharon emerge crying from my cabin. I should probably assign one of the special officers to inform her. I take a walk with her to the torpedo room and give a break to the crewman on duty. Before she can confess to some minor transgression, I give her all the information we possess regarding the events. She has lots of questions; I have few answers. She doesn't cry. I think she holds some faith in the belief that I am wicked enough to furnish her with false news in order to ascertain her ability to work under stress. I remind her that it is critical that she not take any actions that would lead to a leak of the information.

I ask her for more details so I can better understand the purpose of her assignment to *Tekumah*. She reiterates the information concerning enhancement of the targeting capabilities. I receive her assurance that she is not withholding any information from me concerning her mission.

I press for details regarding the nature of the work she is performing to enhance the targeting capabilities of our missiles. She tells me the first upgrade is the addition of the ability to optimize the missile flight path to the target. When we targeted our missiles for the destinations in Iran, we manually programmed the waypoints, which are places where the missile changes direction. This determination is often a complex optimization. It involves plotting a path to avoid radar coverage areas and weapons that can shoot down the missile. It also requires a path that avoids revealing the final destination of the missile until it gives defensive forces little time to react. It also entails masking the submarine's location at the time of launch and other considerations. After the software optimization, the missiles could automatically set their waypoints based upon data submitted regarding the location and capabilities of air defense elements. This enhancement would save time and be more accurate than can be generated under current methods. Second, her assignment involves an update to the missile's guidance system to handle enhanced details made available through Israel's latest generation of spy satellites.

She had completed installation of the software for the Popeye Turbo. Debugging the problems she found required several more days. She could then show me how to program targets under the new scheme. She reports that she has finished the tentative flight programs for several dozen newly optimized "deemed likely" targets and could load these in seconds.

The Harpoon missile software assignment rated a lower priority level. Several of the enhanced capabilities could probably be added to that platform, but it might take at least one hundred work hours, depending upon the difficulty she encounters during the debugging process.

She wants to use one of the boat's communication computers. I inform her that all the times we can receive communications are reserved for the special officers to check for orders and to retrieve the news updates.

Sharon reveals more details regarding her need to access the Internet. Aside from her programming skills, she also has extensive training and experience in "data mining." She hopes to hack into the "secure" servers used by certain Arab and Iranian military communications networks. She would then download information she can transfer to her computer for later analysis. We agree that this aspect of her job should take precedence for now over the missile programs. I briefly recall the special officers to update them in regard to Sharon's duties. I also order them to allow her the access she needs. Now that they know her duties, they have respect for her mission. So they indirectly respect her as well.

Nearly six hours later, the American president announces that there is substantial structural damage in what he called "the isolated area." He explains that an upper atmospheric explosion had generated an electromagnetic pulse. This event has damaged the power grid and most modern electronic devices. He also reveals that radiation in the area is "beyond safe levels."

So we possess an apparent answer for one question. We all know a detonation of a nuclear warhead in the upper atmosphere could cause the pulse described by the American president. It also explains the flash and radiation. The damage area includes much of Israel, the West Bank, and western Jordan. We speculate that Iran had launched a nuclear missile toward Israel. Perhaps, the missile intentionally or accidentally detonated above the center of the affected area. Alternatively, an Israeli Arrow interceptor missile may have detonated the warhead prematurely. We couldn't rule out the involvement of Israel's neighbors. We were suspicious of Syria, which enjoyed close relations with Iran. We reflect on the role the new Pakistani regime may have played in the attack. The second flash presumably would be caused by a second nuclear device. That would explain the damage and radiation at ground level and the mushroom cloud.

We hear the expected range of world opinion. Most of the Arab and Muslim world blames Israel, the only known nuclear power in the region. Their media and leaders express the myth that Israel initiated a nuclear attack against Palestinians and Jordanians. Their theories cannot be inconvenienced with the fact that the damage affects far more Israelis than Arabs.

We know the Jewish residents of the West Bank now face a particularly perilous position. The surrounding Arab communities always outnumbered them. Now, they could not rely upon technology or calls for assistance to forces stationed in Israel. We also fear follow-up attacks against Israel by Iran, Lebanon, Syria, or Egypt.

Yossi speculates that none of Israel's Arab neighbors will launch an attack or allow organizations within their borders to initiate a substantial attack against Israel under these circumstances. He figures the Israeli government would treat any major follow-up attack as evidence of involvement with the initial nuclear attack and completely destroy the nation launching such an attack.

Danny figures that even if an invading force might capture territory, they didn't want to subject their own armies to radiation exposure from dust and debris located within the area they would conquer. He also presumes the invaders don't want the responsibility of taking care of the Arab survivors, who might blame their liberators for irradiating them.

Sergei thinks an invasion is either imminent or under way. Only the loss of communication capability prevents the confirming reports, he declares.

Our fuel situation puts us past the point where we could navigate back around southern Africa to Israel's western coast without receiving additional fuel and food. However, our present position, combined with the range of our Popeye Turbo missiles, leaves us near many potential targets. From the northern Red Sea, we could reach all of Syria with our Popeye Turbo missiles. From the central Red Sea, we could target all of Saudi Arabia. From the Arabian Sea, we could strike much of Iran, and from the Persian Gulf, we could reach the rest. We could deliver missiles to much of Pakistan, including Islamabad, from the northern Arabian Sea.

Our unanswered questions outnumbered the answers. We didn't know the extent of the damage or the cause of it. Was the civilian and military leadership of the nation intact? Why didn't they retaliate with their land-based forces or give us orders to retaliate? Was it because they didn't know who to retaliate against, didn't think they should retaliate, or couldn't retaliate?

CHAPTER 6:
THE ZACHARIAH ORDER

The Israeli navy employs several safety procedures to prevent unauthorized use of our nuclear warheads and missiles. The screening process employed for those individuals whose duties require their access to nuclear warheads is extremely rigorous. There is no "lifetime" clearance granted. The investigators can delve into seemingly private matters even after a crew member has received security clearance. We maintain procedures to severely restrict access to the warheads dockside and at sea. We also use a layer of protection to ensure that even if a thief gained access to the missiles or warheads, they could not be used. Before we leave port, the warheads are enabled for a limited period of time, depending upon the mission. After that time, they must be reenabled. This procedure is to ensure that even if the warheads are stolen, they cannot undergo a thermonuclear reaction at the command of the thief. They would only be useful in the role of a "dirty bomb."

We don't use keys to prearm the warheads. The problem of lost or stolen vehicle keys is a nuisance. Now imagine the keys are those used in connection with a nuclear weapon. A painfully long series of codes, which changes between voyages, must be precisely entered to prearm the warheads. These codes are not carried aboard the boat. They must be received from one of the four individuals I mentioned earlier. After the codes are entered, an iris scan must match the commander and any two of the special officers. This scan even verifies there is a pulse at a rate consistent with consciousness, and the individual must perform a blinking sequence known only to him. In case the commander is incapacitated, we have procedures to enable the successor officer to take his place.

Even without regard to the nature of the warheads, the missiles require procedures designed to prevent targeting by untrained or unauthorized individuals. The coordinates that must be supplied to the weapons program reference a coded modification of GPS coordinates.

We don't require codes, apart from the target information, before we launch the cruise missiles. The weapons are not burdened with this restriction because we are authorized to use them, outfitted with conventional warheads, to protect our boat. There might not be an opportunity to obtain authorization for their use from our headquarters under combat conditions.

The missiles are ordinarily launched from the fire control computer in the control room. A backup function permits a missile launch initiated within the torpedo room. This capability is important in case a fire or accident requires their discharge upon short notice. The flight path of the missiles is programmed only from the control room.

Zachariah is the name of the Israeli military base southeast of Tel Aviv. There, reportedly, Israel maintains 150 of its nuclear warheads and fifty of its Jericho II intermediate range missiles to carry them. The name Zachariah in Hebrew translates as "God remembers with vengeance."

As I informed you earlier, in most instances, we are only permitted to prearm our nuclear warheads upon the authorization of four people. These people sometimes meet in the same room. A well-placed explosive could kill them all in an instant. Despite the enhanced security measures they enjoy, they might also be attacked individually. Succession to their position takes an appointment and approval. There is also the risk that the Israeli-based communication network used to issue orders to the submarine forces could be disabled. Therefore, we employ a backup plan that protects our deterrent capability against even these unlikely risks. The submarine forces can, under specified circumstances, obtain authorization to launch an attack that employs nuclear weapons without the need to establish communications with authorities inside Israel.

There are six military officers attached to Israel's embassies who maintain the authority to make the codes available to our submarine forces. They can only act in the event of a national emergency in which the government of Israel is destroyed or unable to communicate with our strategic forces. These people are the military attachés located at our embassies in Washington DC, London, Paris, Rome, Canberra, and Ottawa.

The geographic diversity and number of individuals has a purpose. In case the city, the embassy building, or the officer is unable to respond for any reason, the other city should be available. You will learn later that only two of these officers can order the use of the weapons.

These embassy officers can undertake secure communications with one another, but they have no access to the powerful transmitters designed to reach our submarines. Their method of communication is by coded messages saved in e-mail accounts. To prove we think of all contingencies, if there is a conflict in orders, there is a ranking system, and we have strong identification and authentication procedures.

This month's coded e-mail communications system simulates a school discussion group. We have previously utilized sports teams and homeowner's association group simulations. The code words are fairly intuitive, and we do not need to refer to notes when we decode them.

We receive information in the form of a draft letter saved

in the Washington DC, Israeli embassy's military attaché's designated e-mail account. It reads:

Attention: all members of the discussion group. (This message is for all deepwater naval forces.)

We have been unable to reach the professor or his assistant. (There has been no communication with civilian or military leaders.)

The library, cafeteria, and all other meeting areas are unavailable because of air-conditioning issues. (The navy bases in Haifa, Eilat, and other areas are considered too "hot" or subject to attack to use.)

We don't know who the publisher of the textbook is. The information is either unknown or is not listed in Samuel's syllabus. (The source of nuclear weapon is unknown. Perhaps the Americans know but do not provide the information.)

We are 90 percent sure the first chapter should be assigned to Ira. (We are 90 percent sure Iran was the launch point of the attack.)

Sara seems to want to take over Jorge's duties. (Syria will probably invade Jordan.)

Esther has been studying late. (Egypt is mobilizing.)

We'll take status, individually, immediately. (Send us your location and condition in the form of draft e-mails.)

Bye now until the seventh. (Your reply e-mails should be in an e-mail account address that matches this address, except that the number in the address should be added to your boat's number times seven.)

* * *

We meet to decide upon our response. We set up our e-mail account and compose a draft response using a word processor. We sign onto the e-mail account long enough to post the draft. It reads:

We are fully rested. (We are fully armed.)

We can do 30–35 pages. (We have thirty to thirty-five days of fuel and food left under normal patrol conditions.)

Our favorite topic is number 155. (Our patrol area is sector 155.)

Later, we checked the draft to ascertain that our contact had accessed it. The reader increased the spacing between paragraphs and saved it.

Our Washington DC, contact, Yariv, has quite a reputation in the American intelligence community. Even the senior American military analysts use Yariv when they need to double-check the logic of their analysis. Reliable rumors held that one senior CIA analyst initiated a "decoy" classification assignment to one Iranian nuclear facility. The CIA relied upon satellite data that showed trucks disappearing into the site and then leaving too quickly to have offloaded anything. Yariv showed the analyst how the building plans for the loading dock at this plant provided greater efficiency than those of other plants. He obtained his own data to show the trucks accelerated from a stop significantly quicker returning from the plant compared to their acceleration on the way to the plant.

Yariv is equally adept at obtaining useful intelligence. He often asks questions that presuppose he already knows the main piece of information he is trying to obtain and simply needs to learn one remaining detail. When the answer comes back that such a detail is not available yet or expresses surprise of his discovery of the item, it provides confirmation that his presupposition is correct.

We did not hear anything further from Yariv. We inform the crew that their e-mails would be delayed because of a security issue. We hear several news reports that American aircraft will be sampling the atmosphere to collect radiation samples. Nuclear forensic scientists could then determine the source of the nuclear material. The analysis would provide a partial answer to our question.

News reports indicate that Egypt had mobilized to prevent

an influx of refugees. Also, we hear that Syrian troops have entered Jordan at the request of the Jordanian government. Their stated purpose is to help with recovery and to "fortify the western border." Several of Israel's embassies are reported to have been attacked and had closed, but the grounds housing the buildings remain secure. The embassies located in the six capital cities with the nuclear weapons authorization codes remain secure.

We hear a new message. It specifies an Iranian launch point for the missiles. The weapons' source is from a Soviet, Pakistani, or North Korean reactor. Those governments or their predecessors or successors could not be tied to the dissemination of the nuclear materials. We also learn that our sister boat, *Dolphin*, was in the midst of an overhaul at the time of the attack. She cannot be sufficiently repaired, outfitted, and manned for combat operations. Our other sister ship, *Leviathan*, is deployed near us but needs assistance because she is short of fuel. We are given an order to meet her in three days.

In the meantime, we receive updates from our embassy contacts that reference the extent of damage to Israel. We hear ranges and estimates: percentage of population dead or presumed dead is estimated at 10 to 20 percent; percentage in immediate danger from wounds and radiation if not evacuated or specially sheltered is 30 to 40 percent; percentage blinded is 2 to 4 percent. I think they give these statistics rather than raw numbers in the belief we will be less affected. They are mistaken.

CHAPTER 7:
TIME FOR A PIRATE STORY

As we head for the rendezvous with *Leviathan*, the dismal news reports continue. There is coverage of deaths from building collapses, failure of power supplies, and lawlessness in areas far from the blast. There are also large-scale rocket attacks from Lebanon, the Gaza Strip, and the West Bank. There is a shortage of clean drinking water. The transportation and communication infrastructure is severely damaged.

Sharon spends most of her time in my cabin. The only reason I go there is to sleep a few feet away from the redundant set of gauges. There are two reasons I can't allow her to work while I sleep. I need time by myself, and I don't want to create the appearance of impropriety. So when I tell her I need to sleep, she copies her files onto a flash drive. She then analyzes the data on one of the boat's computers while I sleep.

Sharon has given me curious stares the past few days. I discover the reason. My crusty sock has been washed and put back in a new location under my mattress. I examine the sock. There are no notes, razor blades, pins, pieces of glass or metal, irritating chemicals, spices, or birth-control devices. It is empty and, considering it is housed on a submarine, dry. It has, to my admittedly dull sense of smell, no odor.

I always go out of my way to assume the innocent explanation regarding someone's behavior. But I must cautiously prepare for other possibilities. I'll suppose that she smelled something that I could not. She might have wanted to politely take care of the problem without embarrassing me. I'm curious regarding the point she tries to make by her actions but not enough so to ask her. I'm better off without hearing any of her potential answers. I don't want her to tell me that the smell bothered her or that I'm harassing her. I don't want to give her ammunition to blackmail me. I can't take the chance she discloses her availability to make its use superfluous. I'll simply find a better place to hide it and clean it myself more often.

On our way to the rendezvous point, I bring the crew up to date concerning the situation back home. To a man, they are all upset and angry but focused. I don't get any impression that they resent that I withheld the news until now. Our navy's psychological screening and crew training deserve some credit. I had prepared to answer a lot of questions, but I don't receive many. I hope the lack of questions does not signify the earlier leak of the information. If I had anticipated the news would have leaked, I would have informed the men sooner. The emotional cost of contemplating uncertainties is always greater than hearing a description of what is known. I order them not to spend any time studying for promotional exams during their time off. Instead, they should rest or review safety procedures.

As we journey near the rendezvous point with *Leviathan*, we work out final details for me to communicate with their commander. We dial back on the power of our transmitters. This action minimizes the chance that our conversation will be overheard outside our immediate area. We have to decide which language to use, in case our signal is picked up. There are a lot of considerations. If we speak Arabic, our radio traffic does not stand out, but if our accents are not good, then we would give away our identity no less than if we spoke Hebrew. If we use English, we have fewer problems with accents. However, if our words are intercepted, there is no delay for translation. If we communicate in Russian, any signal intercepted by the Americans risks unneeded attention. We also must decide which code to use. Usually, we speak "fisherman." This dialect allows for substantial communication without drawing interest from any military eavesdroppers or even most fishermen. We vary the meaning of the jargon according to the calendar, time of day, and location. This scheme ensures even should the eavesdropper decipher the meaning of one conversation, they are no closer to decoding the next one.

We make contact and confirm that *Leviathan* has a severe fuel issue. They also are running low on food. There is no longer any port that would welcome us. The Indian government will not risk increasing tensions with an already on-the-edge Pakistan. I'm sure the Americans will face accusations whether or not they provide us actual assistance.

Since the Americans can't control our target list, I don't think they would participate in enabling us to sustain our nuclear attack capability by providing fuel and supplies. We will have to develop a plan on our own.

We quickly dismiss the idea of sneaking into a port and trying to tap the fuel supply. Our surface fleet will not be operating in our area. The only other option is to pirate fuel from ships at sea. We are now in the north Arabian Sea near Iran and Pakistan. We cannot take the chance that the ships we board might use their radio to contact these nations. We will need to head southwest to the coast of Somalia on the eastern tip of Africa. The ships we encounter might be pirates or merchant traffic. If they are pirates, they won't have anyone to warn by radio regarding our presence. If we have to raid regular commercial traffic, the victim may radio for assistance. Still, if history is a guide, I expect no nation will maintain both the interest and capability to come to the timely assistance of the victim of piracy near Somalia.

We pull alongside *Leviathan* and transfer fuel. We give them most of the Indian military rations. Their commander, Jonah, asks me if I had opened my "special package." I tell him that I expect to wait until our replenishment operation is complete, and he responds he will do the same. We also establish an e-mail communications scheme because after we opened the "special package," we will need to coordinate our activities.

I receive several requests from the men. They want to check on their families in Israel. They know the rules but figure that VOIP (voice over Internet phone) wouldn't present a security risk. They also want to directly check their families' home pages, blogs, or e-mail accounts. I have to deny these requests. These activities directly violate orders. In addition, I couldn't imagine we would receive any news that would help morale. Even if several crew members received good news, it would only heighten anxiety among the others. Also, it is risky to spend time near the surface when it is not absolutely necessary.

There is a request that I can accommodate. The men want to redecorate the missiles in light of the events. I need to decide if we would reconstitute our old teams or create new teams. I could also divide the spaces on the missiles and allow them to express their anger individually. I ask Rami for his opinion, and he suggests we should survey the men. I follow their vote to use the old teams.

This time, we don't offer awards to the participants. The men are not in the mood to participate in a contest that highlights creativity. The artwork takes the form of purely hostile expressions. The expression *"Tisaref be evadon"* (burn in hell) appears in most designs. Mushroom clouds adorn depictions of Tehran, Mecca, and most capital cities in the Arab world. After we finish, the crew appears more focused and businesslike.

On our way to the Somali coast, we also spend several hours rehearsing boarding procedures and making plans. Our scheme prioritizes control of the bridge and particularly the area housing the radio equipment. We also want to position our boats in a precise way. The crew of the boarded ship should believe that the submarine not used in the boarding could attack them. The boarding crew will be composed of men from both boats, which leaves only a skeleton crew to remain aboard each. We know the approximate fuel capacity of different types of ships. The amount of fuel on board at the time we boarded the vessel would be harder to figure. We plan to keep a watch on traffic near the port of Bossaso.

It would be ideal if we can find an anchored ship. It would be quicker and easier for us to board her. A ship that is not moving will be less likely to have the radio manned and might employ fewer crew members as lookouts. We approach several ships within a distance that allows us to determine the type of ship we track. If we need to, we can read the ship and its country of registry through our periscopes. Since we need to remain near the surface to obtain the visual information concerning the ships that cannot be discovered by sonar, we can use the Internet to help us determine the fuel capacity of the ship. In a few instances, the ship's name and its itinerary enable us to estimate the quantity of fuel it holds.

We come across an aid ship that has anchored offshore, out of view of the coast, apparently awaiting clearance from the port. This ship is the best opportunity to obtain food and fuel we can expect. Clear weather conditions would prevent any chance to sneak up on them on the surface. Instead, we would scare them and hope their resulting panic didn't turn violent. We submerge and then surface rapidly, nose up, almost simultaneously with *Leviathan*. I hope that the odd wake this creates does not lead to our detection.

We will provide cover for *Leviathan*, which plans to tie up to the ship for refueling. *Leviathan* has a greater capacity to store fuel than *Tekumah*. They are close to 95 percent empty, and we are still more than 50 percent full. Most of the crew of the aid ship will likely speak only French. The boarding party includes only five crewmen who speak French. The boarding party arrives at the bridge radio quickly. Neither of our boats' radio operators detects any transmission from the ship. Our operation does not suffer from a language barrier, perhaps due to the enhanced clarity of our message provided by our assault rifles. Fortunately, the ship has a larger capacity portable pump than we carry. They probably have to employ it regularly to obtain fuel from primitive port facilities they visit.

Quickly, *Leviathan* takes the fuel needed to top off her tanks. The boarding party also takes rice, previously destined for refugees, in an amount that would feed our crews for the duration of our newly enhanced fuel supply. They also confiscate several memory cards from the cameras they see.

After we submerge and navigate a safe distance away, *Leviathan* shares its fuel and rice. They also return almost all the Indian military meals. Our submarines are now each outfitted with 75 percent of their fuel capacities and enough food for at least forty days. We also settle on boat-to-boat communication procedures for our next round of contacts.

We give the news to Yariv by saving the coded draft message in our designated Internet account.

We hear radio news reports concerning a coup attempt in Saudi Arabia that has killed several members of the royal family. There is no mention of our incident. Perhaps the captain of the aid ship respected our threat to destroy his ship if he reported our attack. Maybe he does not want his ship and crew out of the refugee-relief business while they participate in a lengthy investigation. Or perhaps no one cares.

The news from Israel increases in pessimism. It is now apparent that the earlier reports understated the amount of blast damage and radiation level. Evacuation plans, with few exceptions, were postponed indefinitely. It is under these conditions that I opened my "special package."

CHAPTER 8:
MY "SPECIAL PACKAGE"

I am required to open orders contained in a special package I keep in my safe upon either of two conditions.

I must open the package if our national government is destroyed, and I have reason to believe our government would have authorized the use of nuclear weapons. Our government's policy permits use of nuclear weapons following the use of nuclear weapons against our nation. That policy allows nuclear retaliation for an attack against civilian areas with weapons of mass destruction causing large loss of life. Our leaders may also call for a nuclear response in the event of a substantial destruction of capability of the armed forces to defend population centers. Under this principle, penetration of our cities or the immediate threat of such penetration by foreign armed forces also prompts a nuclear response.

I must also open the package upon the order of our Washington DC, and London military attachés. They are given power to order submarine commanders to open the package under the conditions I told you would trigger a nuclear response. This provision assists the submarine commanders by removing their need to determine independently whether reported events qualify under the doctrine.

On all previous missions, homecoming submarine commanders returned the package to a group of heavily armed military police. They verify the package retains its original seal and then take it into an armored vehicle.

The outside of the package contains bold letters that declare the package may only be opened under conditions specified under Special Order Two. Violation of these procedures constitutes a crime and is subject to severe penalties.

I open the package. A letter covers a series of computer disks and an Old Testament.

I read the letter first. It reads as follows:

Commanding Officer *Tekumah*:

The information included in this package reflects the policy of the national government regarding "Zachariah" operations. The circumstances under which you are reading this document indicate that you have followed established procedures in your determination

That either:

I. Our national government, had it survived, would have reason to and likely would have ordered a retaliatory response involving your boat's nuclear weapons. In this regard, you must have established that:

A. Our government, including its valid successor, is unable to communicate with you; and

B. Our government cannot reasonably be expected to restore communications to you within a strategically timely interval; or

II. Our nation's military attaché in our embassy in Washington DC, USA, or London, England, has ordered you to open this package.

Our government cannot make determinations of proper targets for "Zachariah" operations and communicate them to you. The national government, at the time of this writing, has no reason to determine that an attack against our nation meeting previously communicated criteria would necessarily have been the fault of any particular nation or group. Therefore, you are instructed to determine targets, if any, using the following procedures.

1. You are to follow the orders of our nation's military attaché in our embassy in Washington DC, USA. Those orders are considered invalid unless you and at least two of your special officers make an affirmative determination that they constitute valid and rational orders.

2. If and only if you are without communication with the individual named above, you are instructed to follow the orders of the military attaché in our embassy in London, England. Those orders are considered invalid unless you and at least two of your special officers make an affirmative determination that they constitute valid and rational orders.

3. If you are unable to establish communication with the individuals described under paragraphs one and two or their orders are considered invalid or irrational, you are ordered to select targets, if any, following procedures whose criteria are explained below. In addition, the criteria below shall be used in the determination of whether orders of the individuals named in paragraphs one and two are rational.

A. Your first priority is to prevent the parties responsible for the attack from carrying out further operations against the survivors, if survivors are present in significant numbers and would otherwise survive medical treatment or evacuation.

B. Your second priority is to punish the parties responsible for the attack. Responsible parties constitute the attackers, their inciters, their supplier of weapons, and their supplier of other material or information necessary to undertake the attack. In your identification of parties responsible for the attack, you are permitted to consider potential beneficiaries of an attack against our nation.

C. Under both priorities A and B above, you are to consider the reason our nation's strategic forces have not responded or have responded partially or ineffectively.

If our nation's failure to undertake such operations logically results from our nation's incapacity to strike the responsible nation, in light of damage to our strategic assets or the target nation's range, you may treat such incapacity as support for undertaking an attack.

If our nation's failure to undertake such operations logically results from our leadership, including successors, failing to attain sufficient evidence to make a determination of responsibility, you may treat such uncertainty as evidence that no "Zachariah" operation should be conducted. However, if material, superior evidence, logically unavailable to our leadership is available to you or parties specified in paragraphs 1 and 2 above, then our leadership's failure to attain sufficient evidence to make a determination of responsibility shall not be evidence that such "Zachariah" operation should be conducted.

D. You are to take into account and minimize the damage to any nation for which the large majority population that would be affected by your operations is itself actively hostile to the forces responsible for the attack. For these purposes, the population of majority Islamic nations, other than Turkey, is not considered hostile to attackers associated with that nation.

In addition, you are to consider targets that minimize direct damage to the Jewish communities within the target areas. For these purposes, Jewish populations of Damascus and Tehran are to be given minimal weight. Disks are included to provide Jewish community population information and contact information with community evacuation leaders. It is already realized that the attack against our nation and any "Zachariah" operations are likely to embolden attacks against the Jewish and Israeli communities around the world. You should give minimal weight to any potential increase in these attacks resulting from your specific target selection.

You are to give minimal weight to the chance that your operations would cause additional minimal to moderate casualty attacks against our own nation's survivors. You should give minimal to moderate consideration to the risk that your operations would delay or suspend outside assistance to our own nation's survivors.

E. You are to avoid attacks where the response of the nation you attack poses a substantial risk of a high-casualty counterattack by that nation or other nations or groups allied with it, against a nation with a majority population that is nonhostile to our nation. In this regard, the risk of casualties is to be measured by both an absolute and proportionate-to-population estimation. In addition, you are to ignore the risk that a counterattack will be directed against the United States, if the United States is already hostile to the nation you attack.

4. A disk is enclosed with detailed potential target information including the potential targeted nation's air defenses. You are to select targets and routes within the penetration capabilities of your weapons after taking into account the capabilities of the air defenses en route to the target. Communications with other military and civilian authorities should be minimized to ensure the secrecy of your mission. However, once you have selected your target, you should communicate with armed forces possessing working weapons also within range of your targets to ensure the overall success of your attack and to prevent waste of resources.

5. It is understood that your mission is undertaken during wartime conditions. The course required to complete your mission may increase the risk your boat is subject to operational or combat damage, to an increased risk you will be unable to obtain replenishment of fuel or provisions, and to an increased risk your boat and its crew cannot return to territorial waters

or territory under control of this government. You are to give no weight to these risks.

A. Following completion of your mission, in the event of exhaustion of all weapons capable of attacking distant targets and of all nuclear warheads, in the absence of a reasonable chance or rearmament with such weapons or warheads, you are authorized to deliver yourself and your crew to any location reasonably likely to insure safety. After you have taken these actions to ensure your safety and that of your crew, you are authorized to destroy your boat, in view of this government's determination that the boat will have violated the terms of the agreement with the Federal Republic of Germany for its use. You are ordered to destroy all coded and secret information. You are then specifically authorized to discharge your crew and then yourself from active duty status in the Israeli Defense Forces.

B. If your mission is either (1) cut short under conditions where you are incapable of completing it but there is no risk of capture of your crew or boat; or (2) complete, but your boat retains nuclear weapons, you are to disable such weapons and ensure they remain permanently nonrecoverable. After such undertaking, you may use the procedures in paragraph A above in regard to your crew and your boat.

C. If your mission is cut short and there is an imminent risk of capture of your boat or its crew, you are authorized to use nuclear warheads to prevent such capture only if:

i. The forces attempting your capture are from a nation meriting attack under the criteria above, whether or not you decide to target them, and direct and indirect damage from detonation of the weapon would be substantially limited to combatant armed forces; or

ii. Your defense of the boat would not be possible without nuclear weapons and direct and indirect damage from detonation of the weapon would be substantially limited to combatant armed forces. However, attack under authority of this provision is forbidden against nations that you determine would likely provide substantial assistance to survivors of the attack against our nation, if survivors are present in significant numbers and would otherwise survive medical treatment or evacuation.

In other conditions, you are ordered to destroy your weapons and coded and secret information described above. You are further authorized, but not ordered, to undertake self-destructive acts to prevent capture under circumstances where it is highly likely you or your crew would be killed, imprisoned under conditions where you or they would be subject to torture, or confined for life.

6. These orders and the authorizations contained herein may only be modified, changed, amended, or rescinded upon the order of the undersigned or my successor, the defense minister or his successor, the army chief of staff of his successor, the commander of the navy, or his successor.

We know you will uphold the highest traditions of our nation and our people.

Signed,
Prime Minister of Israel

* * *

I put the letter in my pocket and returned the rest of the package to my safe except for the Old Testament.

I contact the commander of *Leviathan*. For this purpose, we use a password-protected Internet "chat room" for a nonexistent Swedish water polo team. Jonah has already opened his package, which I assume was identical to mine. We draft a joint message for Yariv explaining that we awaited his orders and launch codes. We are notified that we would have a response within twenty-four hours. We soon find out that he will be unable to keep his word.

CHAPTER 9:
ON OUR OWN

Terrorists have the nasty habit of changing their tactics to adapt to our security measures. Miraculously, we usually manage to stay a step ahead of them. Still, when I first heard news reports of the near simultaneous bombings of our embassies in Washington DC, and London, I felt stunned. These buildings featured many layers of protection and safety.

When the detailed news reports reach us, we understand. The terrorists drove a truck bomb to the outer embassy gate. The explosion paved the way for the second truck to exploit the opening to make its way to a point nearer the building. The second truck blew up, killing the security personnel who had already engaged it. The third truck drove to the main building and exploded. In Washington DC, while the first ambulance left the site, a fourth truck, parked a block away on the route to the hospital, detonated remotely. The London operation did not employ a fourth truck.

We don't know with certainty whether Yariv or our London contact were among those suffering critical burns, the missing, or the dead, but we know that no person in those categories would be in a position to issue orders.

I have always imagined that if the day would come for *Tekumah* to launch nuclear weapons, my role would be merely to execute the decisions of others who would have selected the targets. The real responsibility for the events would belong to others. I had imagined that I would receive a list of targets and be able to convince myself of the skillful performance by target analysts. I pictured the burden carried by the man who would have given such an order, even in retaliation.

So Jonah and I now hold a much greater burden of sole responsibility for selection of targets for our missiles. Our combined ages probably barely equal that of some of the candidates for the office of prime minister of Israel in the last elections.

I remember going out on dates and wanting to take along contraceptives even though I knew it unlikely I would need them. I reasoned that if I did need them, I did not expect to have the time to leave a "hot" situation and purchase them. In light of the security problems at our embassies, I feel caution requires that we obtain the codes now, even though we have not decided upon targeting information. I aim to avoid the distraction of communications with the embassies while I might need to manage my other duties during "heated" events.

Having to purchase contraceptives is embarrassing. It is a statement that concerns intent to undertake the most intimate and private activity. In asking for the codes, I'm asking for something that enables retribution against millions of people—many of whom are innocent—for the harm inflicted upon other millions. I'm asking for the power of God.

Leviathan and *Tekumah* feature unique nuclear weapon-enabling codes, so Jonah and I each must ask for our own boat's codes. I draft my letter to the officers at the remaining four embassies "Under the authority of the prime minister ..."

Diplomats tend to be, well, diplomatic. They don't want to believe that force should be needed. The military attachés aren't diplomats. They possess a better understanding of our needs. I'm sure the attacks against the other embassies place emotion behind their decision. So Jonah and I didn't have to wait long to receive the power of God. After I lock the codes away in my safe, I retrieve my own "in case of death" file where we keep personal information needed in case one of us dies at sea. I add information that would enable Naftali to figure out the combination to my safe.

Jonah and I next have to determine how long to wait for orders from Tel Aviv, Washington DC, or London before we conclude that we need to act on our own. We learn that Yariv is among the "missing." There is no chance that his missing means that he was outside the area for some reason. It signifies that he almost certainly lies dead, his body underneath a pile of rubble. We agree that it is unlikely anyone can be pulled from a collapsed building after a few days and be expected to survive with their senses. Our London contact is in critical condition. His prospect for a recovery to a degree sufficient to contact us appears unlikely. The other factor driving our decision is that the fuel and supplies we need to conduct operations continues to dwindle. I accept Jonah's idea of allowing seventy-two hours from the time of the reported embassy bombings for contact before we will act on our own initiative. In the meantime, we will make our own plans for targets and tactics. *Leviathan* carries the same offensive payload supplied to *Tekumah*.

We first must decide upon the list of targets. We will then decide how many weapons they merit and how to divide them up. Later, we will move forward to the issues of finding a relatively safe launch point or points and then to the timing of the attack. We also want to consider if we should issue any statement of explanation justifying our retaliation. If we do issue a statement, we need to decide where to "publish" it ahead of the attack. Such publication would prevent others from fraudulently claiming responsibility for our actions after the attack occurs. But such notice must not give away our position or allow time for heightened missile defense.

I don't have to consult with the special officers under the terms of my orders. I seek advice from them for many reasons. First, I want them to see that I am following procedures. They will appreciate that my decisions are not merely rational but necessary. They will then be able to sign off, or in reality, "blink-off" during the prearming of the warheads. Second, there is too much data for me to handle alone. Third, I know they received instruction in this area and could keep secrets. Fourth, they are less busy than the rest of the other officers in the crew.

I'll send summaries of my thoughts periodically to Jonah. I'll want to know what he has determined as well. We synchronize our times to run near the surface so we can communicate several times a day.

We start with a brief review from Yossi regarding the nature of war under Jewish law. We recall that all Israeli soldiers are taught a code known under the words "*tohar haneshek*" (purity of arms). The code is taught during the beginning of weapons training. The IDF servicemen and women are instructed to use their weapons and force solely for the purpose of their mission, only to the necessary extent, and must maintain their humanity even during combat. IDF soldiers may not use their weapons and force to harm human beings who are not combatants or are prisoners of war. They will do all in their power to avoid causing harm to their lives, bodies, dignity, and property.

We move on to the discussion of the difference between "*milchemet mitzvah*" (mandatory war), "*milchemet reshut*" (optional or discretionary war), and "*milchemet brera*" (war of choice). We are not equipped to debate ancient interpretations of Jewish law. After half an hour of discussion, we come to a simple agreement. Our attack scheme will conceptually fit *milchemet mitzvah* principles if our purpose is to protect the survivors from further attacks and not to merely punish the attackers. Technically, our motives will be to deter future attacks by showing Israel's enemies our ability and willingness to punish the present attackers. It is time to discuss the details.

Sergei thinks our overall scheme should be to attack distant targets simultaneously. This plan implies the use of more than a single platform of attack. He suggests we should make our initial attack using fewer warheads than the known capacity of our type of submarine. He argues this strategy provides enhanced deterrence against any follow-on attacks against Israel. We would prove each vessel to have participated and that we retained further capability. Our capability would last for only a few additional weeks. However, an adversary could never disregard our potential to strike unless and until our boats and their weapons could be accounted for.

Right away, Danny wants to jump to the issue of how to cause the most damage to the Islamic and Arab world. He wants us to undertake an attack over a sustained period of time, but at the same hour of the day each time. He wishes that even those residents of cities not attacked suffer widespread panic while they wait their turn to face our onslaught. This concept provokes a hostile response from Noam that we need to obtain more information before we play God. The debate regarding the nature of God that follows undoubtedly ranks with those conducted through the ages and within most every civilization, but I need to steer our discussions back to relevant issues.

Yossi gives us a procedure we easily agree to follow. Our first step will be the elimination of "substantially blameless" nations from the list of potential adversaries. Obviously, the only continents with potential targets are Europe, Africa, and Asia. We quickly eliminate all European nations except for Russia and all African nations except for Egypt. The only non-Middle Eastern nations within Asia that remain open for discussion are North Korea and Pakistan.

We then moved forward to the elimination of nations for more practical reasons. In the case of the non-Middle Eastern nations, we recognize that practical problems eliminate any chance of attack. An attack against Russia, if traced to Israel, would quickly eliminate the survivors. Also, our submarines do not maintain the unrefueled range to reach Vladivostok from the Sea of Japan, much less attack St. Petersburg from the Gulf of Finland. North Korea could not be attacked for several reasons. The distance to its waters compares with the distance to Vladivostok. In addition, its people suffered under the effects of a dictator who would probably attack nonhostile South Korea, Japan, or the United States. Ultimately, Russia and North Korea are too distant from our "primary targets." A voyage to these waters would leave us out of range of our primary targets for many weeks.

Pakistan is certainly more within our reach but would likely counterattack nonhostile India in addition to Israel. In the absence or more direct proof of their involvement, we eliminate that nation from consideration for attack.

We eliminate any Arab nations that have not provided recent substantial material and financial support to our enemies. Iraq falls under this exemption in light of the present government's discontinuance of the policies of Saddam Hussein. However, even if the government were proven to have cooperated with the attack, there is another reason we could not attack Iraq. I told you earlier that the Israeli navy was an indirect beneficiary of the attacks ordered by the late Saddam Hussein against our nation. Now, his overthrow by the Americans and the insurgency he inspired, or his absence enables, keeps large numbers of American armed forces deployed in Iraq. We could not strike Iraq because of this continuing deployment.

We decide to determine those parties responsible for the attack. We do not need to spend a lot of time in a debate regarding the responsibility of Iran. We read the communication that concludes with 90 percent certainty that the launch point originated from Iran. The rhetoric of the government, their assistance to terrorist armies fighting us, and their weapons program are strong pieces of evidence. We also recall our own adventure in the Persian Gulf, including the long hours with the nuclear weapons installed. Although I am still the only individual with official knowledge of the launch probabilities during that operation, I'm sure the rest of the crew realizes that we came close to launching our missiles.

So I know our government prepared to make a preemptive and, perhaps, nuclear attack against Iran. That mission demonstrated our government's thinking at that moment in time. They undertook plans to prevent an attack and save lives. Now that an attack has occurred, the nature of targets for prevention of further attack and for retaliation necessarily reflected different criteria. The American counterattack after the mine incident probably obliterated most of the nuclear facilities. Without a report from the ground, we could not attain assurance, however.

Most of the officers appear fatigued. I should take a break as well. I can't afford for my judgment to become impaired. I initiate a six-hour break before we address the issues that will surely prove more controversial. I communicate with Jonah. He has already selected specific targets in Iran but isn't willing to abandon the idea of an attack against Pakistan. I ask him if the chance that Pakistan supplied the weapon troubles him. He replies that finding they did supply the weapon would prove conclusive, but their other activities may constitute sufficient "responsibility." The risk to India doesn't bother him. He implies that India might want to join the attack to reduce the risk of attack from a counterstrike.

I don't know what bothers me the most regarding Jonah's idea. He has a low threshold for determining responsibility. He is willing to violate orders and risk tens of millions of lives in India. He has the power to trigger a war between two nuclear powers. I make my rounds on the boat and then send a message to our remaining contacts. I want to know if there would be any more definitive determination of the source of the weapon and its launch point. I also ask for an updated report regarding the damage to Israel. I then fall asleep while reviewing the maintenance logs.

CHAPTER 10:
FOUR ISRAELIS, FIVE OPINIONS

The crew appears increasingly distracted. I ask them to give me messages to forward to an Internet message box for our embassies. Hopefully, their expressions would enable them a degree of closure and some of the comfort one receives from communicating with family. The embassies would undertake to locate their families and forward the messages. I have to read them for security reasons. Mainly, they sent messages of love and reassurances. Many writers include direct or indirect statements that the reader could be proud of *Tekumah*'s role in exacting vengeance against Israel's attackers. Several include what seem to be references to places to meet outside Israel. I cleanse the messages of any identifiers, eliminating references to the boat, our future plans, and anything with potential to constitute a "code word." I code the messages and send them to the box for the embassies.

We resume our discussions of targets. We had completed the easy decisions concerning nations that should not be struck and determination of Iranian responsibility. There is a saying, "Two Jews, three opinions." It is almost our national sport to argue every idea. Before we start, I remind everyone that the decision regarding targets is solely my own. I ask them for ideas and advice, and while I will listen, I am not bound to follow their ideas. I appeal to them to treat everyone else with respect even while we criticize each other's ideas.

Danny starts our discussions with an impassioned speech contrasting the Holocaust with the current attack. During the Holocaust, the Jewish people did not have a nation in which to take refuge. Of equal importance, we didn't enjoy a national armed force to use to defend ourselves or punish our attackers. He also makes the point that our government has long undertaken acts of retribution. He lists the capture, trial, and execution of Adolf Eichmann, the murder of the terrorists responsible for the murder of the Olympic athletes at Munich, and numerous raids against the leadership of the PLO, Hezbollah, Hamas, and other groups. Noam counters that in all these cases, our government limited its response. The Israeli government ordered revenge against only those directly responsible for ordering or committing violent acts. Attacks were not ordered against entire populations, and great care was made to minimize damage to noncombatants. Yossi responds that most, if not all the Arab world, enabled the attack against Israel through their policies and financial support of the attackers. He says the natural outcomes of their actions led to the attack by Iran, and they undoubtedly celebrate it. Sergei adds that the United States' action in Afghanistan and Iraq, when neither of these nations had attacked the United States, should be instructive. He also points out the losses from allied bombing of German and Japanese cities in World War II.

"How many civilian casualties did the Americans suffer from German or Japanese attacks during World War II? How many civilian casualties did the Americans inflict?" Sergei asks.

Noam argues back that our moral standards must remain higher than those of the United States. Danny answers that those soft policies failed to deter an attack against us.

I want to return the discussion to an issue that should lead to an agreement. I remind the group that there may not be many weapons left over after our attack against Iran. I want to focus the discussion to the specific issues regarding how many weapons we would need to use against Iran and how to prioritize targets.

Instead of agreement, this discussion brings out long arguments concerning the efficacy and justification of attacking nuclear facilities, missile sites, oil facilities, ports, military bases, "leadership" targets, or Islamic holy sites. Noam states that threatening cities has a deterrent value. He explains that when deterrence has failed, they can no longer be attacked.

I privately speculate how he attained his position with his views concerning the subject of permissible use of nuclear weapons.

We examine the efficacy of targeting Iran's fixed missile sites. The missiles launched from fixed sites could carry both nuclear and nonnuclear weapons of mass destruction. However, the American attack against these facilities should have destroyed them. It is doubtful the Iranians could have rebuilt these facilities during the interval since the attack. We couldn't be sure of accomplishing any meaningful goal with an attack against these locations.

Iran's mobile missile force remained within range to reach Israel with a chemical, biological, or radiological payload. We did not have any prospect of obtaining up-to-date satellite information to target them, however.

We have no way of knowing the location of the leadership on an hour-by-hour basis. We know of areas of the country where their popularity is strongest. However, our job is not to overthrow the Iranian government. Furthermore, such an attack would likely rally support for the government.

Airfields might be employed to launch an attack against Israel. The Americans likely rendered them unusable, but their attacks could merely delay their reconstruction and eventual use. The American forces in Iraq should prevent any flyover from Iran toward Israel. We don't have the same level of confidence if the Iranian air force attack route passes through Saudi Arabia, Persian Gulf nations, or Syria.

We need to review our goals. Should we aim to cripple the oil-based economy of Iran? This type of attack would deprive not only its population but also the rest of the world of its oil resources. Should we kill off the civilian population, specifically those residing in Tehran?

We recognize that destroying the Iranian oil production and distribution capacity would benefit the remaining oil-producing nations. Our attack would increase oil revenues to nations that likely celebrated Iran's attack. However, we think such an attack would be a just punishment and serve to deter other nations. A strike against port and pipeline facilities would delay utilization of the Iranian oil reserves for a long period.

We recognize that much of the population does not like the leadership but deem an attack against the populace morally acceptable. A single weapon would not kill everyone living in the Tehran area but would cause enough damage to ensure sufficient retribution. We determine the top targets. In total, our target list would expend twenty missiles primarily against military and oil facilities and leave eight missiles unused between us and *Leviathan*. We figure we would need these weapons in case air defense or a malfunction in any of the twenty missiles prevented their detonation. Otherwise, they could serve in the function of a continuing deterrent force to a counterattack or might be used against any new attacking nation.

I call another break and then communicate once more with Jonah. I ask him if he received orders to prepare to launch his missiles near the time we aborted our attack. I expect any such orders involved an attack confined to Iran. I could use this fact to help talk him out of a wider attack.

Leviathan patrolled the Red Sea the day of our abortive launch from the Gulf. Jonah has an interesting interpretation of *Leviathan*'s mission that day. He thinks an Israeli Air Force attack against Iran, supported by midair refueling, was planned. He suggests the route would have taken the bombers above the Red Sea and then over Saudi Arabia. He thinks that permission of the Saudi government might not have been obtained or could not be revealed. His missiles, equipped with conventional warheads, were targeted against radar installations and airfields in Saudi Arabia along such a route. His launch probability was also designated "high," equivalent to our own.

If authorized, his strike would have protected the striking force and aerial refueling tankers. At minimum, it would have supplied the Saudi government with evidence to support the claim that they tried to attack the Israeli Air Force and thus lacked complicity in the attack against Iran.

Jonah has selected twenty-eight targets for us to divide. I don't want to know, but I have to know what his list contains. He includes a few military and oil installations in Iran along with Tehran. I am only mildly shocked to learn that he didn't confine his list to Iran. He includes populous cities in Pakistan, Saudi Arabia, Egypt, and Syria.

I did not maintain a substantial relationship with Jonah before this incident. I know a person never really knows someone unless they have seen that person under stress. Hearing of an attack against your nation is not an excuse for irrational behavior. We were selected and trained to not only carry out orders but to make our own rational decisions.

There are only a few ways to reconcile my differences with Jonah. I could agree to his target list, he could agree to mine, or we could act semi-independently. My interpretation of our orders does not permit an attack against any nation other than Iran. I don't think I can influence him to adopt my list. If we acted semi-independently, the only benefit would be to coordinate enough to make sure we didn't "make the rubble bounce" by attacking identical targets.

CHAPTER 11:
DECISION TIME

On a submarine, there are many things the commander does not know and lots of men who hope he does not find out. I make it a habit to walk around the boat, look at the men and equipment, listen, and ask direct questions.

It is a good thing that I'm noticed "sleepwalking" around the boat. Naftali tells me I had made my rounds four times without stopping or focusing. The men are asking one another what I am looking at and whether I feel well. I "wake up" and summon Naftali to my cabin. Naftali had previous service with Jonah and knew him better than I did. I show him my orders and explain the differences in our attack plans. I then ask him to describe Jonah and his motivations.

Naftali advises me that Jonah deserves his characterization as a strong-willed commander. He also describes Jonah as more religious than most submariners. He discloses Jonah's rumored investigation and subsequent clearance of charges relating to involvement with extremist anti-Arab groups. I ask him if he knows what could be motivating Jonah or what could change his mind regarding his attack plan. He advises me that Jonah's commitment to military service held a strong grip over him. His religious commitment remained stronger, however. Jonah would follow orders, but his primary obligation would be to protect Jewish Israel.

Naftali informs me that Jonah always remained informed of *Leviathan's* position at sea with respect to which potential targets entered or left missile range. Jonah told Naftali that even if his missiles couldn't deter the present attackers, they could eliminate the next generation. Jonah could also sell his ideas and wouldn't have a problem persuading the special officers to follow his initiatives.

He advises me that under these conditions, there is only one way the Jonah he remembers would change his mind. He would have to receive specific orders from recognized authorities directing him to attack particular targets.

I don't maintain much hope that our chain of command would materialize to issue orders. I must find another plan.

I convene the meeting with the special officers and update them regarding my communication with Jonah. Danny appears validated that Jonah wants to cast a wider field of responsibility for the attacks against Israel. Noam is adamant in his desire to prevent such an attack. Sergei and Yossi don't think what the other boat's commander decides has much to do with our mission.

Another round of discussions changes my mind regarding my original plan to retain unused missiles. Our launches will give away our position. Iranian or other hostile forces would have a decent chance of discovering our location before we could reestablish our stealth. We would not have a good opportunity to obtain accurate reports of the success we enjoyed against particular targets such that we would be able to retarget locations where our missiles fail to reach the target and detonate their missiles. So there was not much point in retaining unused missiles. As long as *Tekumah* remains operational, we would continue to deter our adversaries through the risk that we somehow overstocked our designed missile storage complement or were resupplied. My decision does not depend on my competitive nature and Jonah's use of fourteen missiles.

I review the maintenance logs with Rami. I can sense that I am distracted. I excuse myself and retire to my cabin to find a pad of paper. I make out a list of goals. First, I want *Tekumah* to engage in a successful delivery of missiles against important Iranian targets. Second, I want to prevent Jonah from widening our counterattack to non-Iranian targets. Third, I want to maximize our chances of survival after the missile launches. I want to leave us in a situation where we have a reasonable chance of safely making port in Eilat.

I take another sheet of paper to make a list of methods to achieve my goals and the chance of success using them: establish communications with any authority that could issue orders to attack only Iranian targets (difficult); persuade Jonah to limit his attacks (very difficult); deceive Jonah into believing that he had received such an order to limit his attacks (difficult and illegal); accept Jonah's target list and divide the targets so that *Tekumah* is assigned to attack the non-Iranian targets and *Leviathan* to attack the Iranian targets and then "fail" in our mission (illegal and difficult).

Several of my means to achieve my goals will eliminate other means if I fail. In other words, if I fail to trick or persuade him, it would make Jonah distrust anything else I tell him. I must decide my main approach and alternatives in a logical order.

I return to Rami and the maintenance logs better able to focus this time. I then draft and send a message to our embassy contacts to request they help me to persuade Jonah to limit his attack to Iranian targets. I take my final nap before I must make my final judgment.

At our next ascension to communications depth, I have responses from the attachés. The Paris contact informs me that there have been many attacks against Jews in France following the attack against Israel. The media have greatly underreported their number and severity. He not only approves of Jonah's target list but wants to add Algeria and other Arab nations obviously not involved in the attack against Israel.

Our Ottawa liaison informs me that he couldn't issue any orders authorizing or preventing an attack. He adds that both boats should carry out their last orders until proper authorities materialize.

Our Rome attaché remains occupied with rescue operations but manages a terse response stating he does not have the authority to alter the prime minister's orders.

The most help I receive is from our Canberra contact. He offers to contact Jonah to urge a delay in launching counterattacks. He would ask him for a three-day postponement. This deferral would allow completion of the current round of "assistance operations." I don't think that our attacks will begin before that time in any event. So I'm on my own.

I review the missile launch and prearming procedures and programs. I'm looking for any opportunity to formulate a plan to allow me to remotely affect *Leviathan*. The nuclear weapons would fail to work if disabled by the antitampering provisions. I already described the iris scan and blinking procedures. Once the nuclear warheads were prearmed and launched with the cruise missiles, they could not be disarmed. The missiles ran a program to arm the warheads under specified conditions involving the attainment of certain altitudes, distance traveled, and minutes of operation of their jet engines, which would be programmed before launch. Once armed, they would detonate upon the earlier of two events: arrival at the programmed GPS coordinate or breaking of a series of wires—think fuses—connected to the detonator. The wires were weak enough to break in the event of a crash or impact by an intercepting missile or antiaircraft artillery, but strong enough to withstand normal flight.

I could not create a fake message to give it the appearance

of an authorized message from Israel, Washington DC, or London. Our military communication security procedures were purposely too strong for even an insider to bypass. I do not expect to persuade Jonah that I had adopted his target list and could be given the non-Iranian targets.

I have to attempt to directly persuade him. I make another list of considerations I might use to appeal to Jonah's practical side. Only Iran appeared to threaten further nuclear attack. Our highest priority is to disable their military and nuclear capabilities. For us to achieve this goal would expend most of the twenty-eight weapons available between both submarines. Attacks against Pakistan would provoke a nuclear response against Israel. An attack against Syria and Egypt might end or, at minimum, delay or diminish the relief efforts now benefiting Israelis. An attack against Saudi Arabia might provoke Western powers or the Russians into attacking Israel to protect the remaining oil supply from further attacks. Surely dozens of Israel's nuclear weapons must have survived. If the military wanted to attack Egypt or Syria, they could have found a way to deliver those weapons by now. Both those nations maintain substantial nonnuclear WMDs, conventional artillery, and missiles. Each would cause mass casualties with their counterattack.

I know I have already mentioned Jonah's political orientation. I should enlighten you with my own. There really is no political party that describes the way I feel. My politics stem from what is practical. Theories don't matter to me; results do. Haifa, for a time, was known under the moniker "Red Haifa." The many dock workers and trade union members who participated in political movements earned the city this nickname. What a beautiful system communism would be if only people were wired differently. Communism or socialism may make people feel good when they proclaim their support of such a system, but these systems simply don't succeed when tried with modern people. People are too greedy to be productive under such a system. Pure capitalism doesn't work either, of course. You have to prevent extreme wealth differentials and provide social services, while leaving incentives for the society and individual to remain productive.

Haifa has a substantial Arab population of about 9 percent. My father's shop employed a large number of Arab Israeli mechanics. Many are good people and make good neighbors. I'm sorry that there are families who can't reunite. I'm sorry their brethren choose to follow or fall under the control of such poor leaders. However, I think it is pretty well demonstrated that you cannot take actions that allow an Arab to think you are weak, or you invite aggression. This notion applies in relations between the Arabs in addition to dealings with outsiders. Despite this, it is not practical to remain at a state of war with hundreds of millions of Arabs. So you must take calculated chances to make peace, provided you don't increase the incentives for war.

CHAPTER 12:
WE DON'T HAVE TIME FOR A "WHODUNIT"

I am still adding to my list when Noam comes to me with the news that Riyadh, Saudi Arabia, has suffered a nuclear detonation. Noam thinks that Jonah has preempted our efforts to alter his target list. I am baffled, and then I receive a message from Jonah that leaves me at a complete loss.

It starts, "I thought we agreed to coordinate. Why didn't you attack the Iranian military first?"

I start to respond that we didn't make the attack. Then I consider that I might want Jonah to think we did make the attack. He might accept a list of targets limited to Iran in the belief that we could be trusted to attack the other nations. No, this chance at deception could not succeed. I wrote back that we did not bring about the attack.

I convene the group to discuss the issue. Several theories involve Israel. They think *Dolphin* has put to sea and made the attack. They speculate that Israel has used a surface ship, perhaps nonmilitary, but capable of launching a cruise missile. Perhaps the Israeli Air Force is at long last responding to the attack with missiles or aircraft. Maybe a truck driver managed to carry the bomb across at least fifteen hundred kilometers of desert roads and sand. Perhaps the detonation stemmed from a preplanted "doomsday" device. None of these theories seemed likely possibilities. No logic explained why the first target selected by Israel should be the nonimmediate threat imposed by the Saudi Arabian capital.

Pakistan, with its new radical government and two thousand kilometer range nuclear missiles, maintained the capability for an attack, and the rulers had sufficient motive. The Pakistanis would see the Saudi government as too decadent and beholden to the Americans and Europeans. Wouldn't it be more sensible for them simply to overthrow the Saudi monarchy or threaten them into submission rather than to destroy a city?

The stronger argument focuses on the benefit that accrues to Iran from the attack. The Iranian regime embodies an economic and spiritual rival to the Saudi monarchy. This attack might represent the follow-up to the earlier failed coup attempt. Also, it could give Iran the chance to rise to the position of chief defender of the Islamic faith. Iran might "protect" Saudi Arabia by renewing its attack against Israel. The disruption in the Saudi oil supply would greatly increase the Iranian regime's oil revenue when prices reacted.

We might never obtain the answers to the questions for us to make sense out of this event. Was there a claim of responsibility? Was the detonation at ground level or above? If the delivery system was by missile or aircraft, did radar or satellite data record a trajectory? What nation provided the source of the radioactive material used to make the bomb? Clearly, there would be no dependable answers for a long time. We couldn't wait for confirmation of our premise of Iranian responsibility for the attack against Saudi Arabia.

When I discuss the situation with Jonah, we both comprehend the urgency in making our strikes against Iran. If we are quick enough, we hope to prevent Iran from "answering" its own attack against Saudi Arabia with a new strike against Israel. We are both in the Arabian Sea, but *Leviathan* is closer to the Gulf of Oman than we are. We finish our attack plan in the Swedish water polo team chat room. *Leviathan* would initiate the attack at the moment she journeyed within range of all fourteen targets. Jonah agrees to modify *Leviathan's* target list to prioritize fixed missile sites, areas that generally contain mobile missiles, and military headquarters. We would follow with a strike against the most hardened nuclear sites that the Americans may not have destroyed along with air bases. We would then attack the oil ports and pipelines. Lastly, we would destroy the city of Tehran.

Jonah will take his submarine into the gulf for only the third time in its history. I had already informed him that we were tracked very well by helicopters, presumably operated by the Americans, during our last excursion there. I would like to know the disposition of the naval forces he finds there, but I know he will be too busy to update me. Also, by the time we arrive in the waters he once occupied, the situation will likely have changed.

Jonah should be fortunate enough to arrive at his launch zone shortly after dawn and during conditions where there will still be a substantial fog blanket. This weather condition should make it harder for satellites to determine the launch point.

If we operated at communications depth, we could receive the signal from any UAVs launched and directed by *Leviathan*. These are unmanned aerial vehicles, basically sophisticated model planes with cameras, which are used to keep a bird's-eye view on the surface. The information we obtain would be useful in identifying surface contacts. But the trade-off from the required operation at such a shallow depth would be foolish. I am already nervous regarding the need to operate near the surface to recharge our batteries after we pass the Strait of Hormuz and before the launch. We will not be able to receive updates from Jonah.

As we near the Gulf of Oman, I want to complete prearming

the warheads. Sharon had requested that she be allowed to observe how the procedures worked. I don't think she realizes that there will not be any communication to anyone interested in future improvements to these procedures. This is a one-time-only event. I follow protocol and decline her request. I promise her that I will give her a briefing later.

I don't need all the special officers to perform the prearming. I can't transform the prearming into something resembling an execution where all participate, but none knows who fires the blank. I have to pick only two of the special officers. I decide to include Noam. Since he is the most dovish, his participation should serve to insulate the rest of us from remorse. Maybe I simply want to force him to adopt the majority viewpoint. He does not object. I also select Yossi. He is the most religious of the special officers. I think his faith will serve to alleviate any feelings of guilt he might feel when he reflects back upon his participation.

With the prearming out of the way, we are able to launch quickly if needed. In the worst case of early detection, the longer-range Popeye Turbo missiles can still reach important Iranian targets from here. We approach the Strait of Hormuz and empty our waste tanks. This time, I order tape applied to the valves that empty the toilet's waste. The wall near the valve features painted instructions that say, "Empty tanks only when authorized." But I still don't trust Sharon in this regard.

Our battery condition dictates that we ascend to a depth that allows us to raise our snorkel and start our diesels. We also raise the communications mast. We do not receive a signal from *Leviathan's* UAV. There is no communication from Israel or the embassies.

Sharon is unable to receive infrared imagery from satellites orbiting above Iran to determine the success of *Leviathan's* attack. However, she intercepts military communications— presumably American—to give me the detailed results of *Leviathan's* attack. Nine missiles detonated at or near the target. Three others detonated within ten kilometers of the target—apparently after antiaircraft fire triggered the detonator. The last two detonated over Iranian territory but not near the target or heavily populated areas.

We are within range of all but four of the targets and actually within range of two others, if we reprogrammed the missile flight paths for a more direct route. Most of our checklist is complete. The missile flight paths and conditions for arming the warheads were already programmed and checked twice.

We are watching the charge on the batteries increase. One final check of the news brings a summary of the American president's major announcement. In that speech, he announces that to ensure an end to the fighting, any further attacks by any nation in the region using WMDs would meet with that nation's destruction.

So our position is similar to the prizefighter who has a chance to land a last blow to his opponent a second after the bell sounds to end the round. We risk more than disqualification from a fight, however.

While I don't mind navigating dangerous waters if I am in control, I feel nervous when I am a passenger on a car, bus, train, or airplane. In the same way, it bothers me that we are now supposed to put our national security in the American president's promise. Unfortunately, we don't have Yariv to give us an interpretation of the president's promise. I'm sure Yariv also would have given us his conclusion regarding which nation was responsible for the attack against Riyadh.

I keep a disk in my safe that generates a grid that provides the estimated casualty range for each target under variables involving yield of the weapon, altitude of detonation, and time of day. I figure if we avoid mass casualties and the oil resources, the American president will find a way to overlook the timing of our attack. I spare the dockworkers and an air base near a city and millions of residents of Tehran.

Even with our updated target list, we still have a problem.

We need to launch soon if we expect the president to wink at our violation. A quick launch of four to eight missiles would send several messages. First, if there are experts counting, they will determine that the total number of missile strikes between *Leviathan* and us exceeds the number of missiles typically stocked on an Israeli submarine. *Leviathan's* targets and ours included points considerably inside the Iranian border and well inland. The target locations combined with the absence of a ballistic missile trajectory would confirm the operations of two vessels capable of launching these weapons. Again, counting normal weapons capacity, authorities would know that at least one submarine must retain unused weapons.

We reprogram eight missiles to target nuclear facilities and air bases in the most unpopulated areas. I reject trying to retarget the two sites that *Leviathan* failed to strike. I must assume the same air defense that knocked down the missiles used for the first strike would prove effective against our second strike unless we configured an updated flight path. We did not possess the data or the time to perform such a reconfiguration. The security provisions allow us to change the flight path after they are prearmed without requiring reentry of codes provided the target is within a preapproved range of GPS coordinates.

The president should be happy that we will thwart any use of these facilities against his bases in Iraq or other oil exporting nations. The list of casualties from reprogramming brings the projected casualty total from *Tekumah's* attack down from the six to eight million range to fifteen to forty-five thousand. Even the upper range of those numbers is less than the fatalities of the atomic bombings of Hiroshima or Nagasaki. The lower range of those numbers is probably not much more than Japanese civilian deaths from America's continued conventional bombings of Japanese cities between the Nagasaki attack and the Japanese agreement to surrender five days later. And remember, the Americans fought an enemy whose defense of their nation was ordered to continue against all odds by their leaders. Our fight is against an enemy who in many cases did not require their leaders to persuade them to offer their lives. They looked forward to sacrificing their lives for the cause of our nation's destruction rather than defense of their nation. I don't think the American president's notification will prove a deterrent to further attacks against Israel. We are destroying Iranian facilities that might be used to manufacture weapons or launch an attack. This assault is not retribution but prevention.

We are already in a decent spot from which to launch. No aircraft or helicopters are detected. However, we recently passed two oil tankers heading in the opposite direction. Even if crew notices the launch behind them or spots the vapor trail rising into the sky, it shouldn't matter. We will already effectively give away our location by firing the missiles. It is literally now or never.

CHAPTER 13:
NOT SO UNDETECTABLE

I t is light outside. The sky is partly cloudy. The two tankers are only a few kilometers away. We arrive at periscope depth. There is a fog bank nearby. I chance surfacing long enough for Ziv to assemble and release a UAV. We then submerge to periscope depth.

I have some requests from the crew I am required to deny. Several want to leave their assigned stations so they may either view my order of the launch or actually be present in the torpedo/missile room when we launch the missiles. I can't allow this deviation from procedures. We can't risk interference or distraction. Also, they need to remain focused on their duties to help us escape from the Gulf.

I'm sure the purpose of all the training we perform is to make our launch second nature. Still, we all know that this event is different from simulations and training. I don't have second thoughts concerning whether to perform the launch. To the extent I think about those on the receiving end, I imagine they are all either celebrating their past attack or planning a follow-up. I also imagine that some time in the future another nation's leader will consider another attack against our people.

The planner of the attack will recall today's events, and the attack will be cancelled.

I am almost surprised that we remain undetected long enough to fire the second group of four missiles. In planning our escape, I reject the thought of trying to follow underneath and behind one of the nearby tankers while it journeys toward the mouth of the Gulf. I think the vessel might be diverted. The captain might be instructed to find a safe port until what was now reported under the news headline of the "Attack on Iran" had ended. In addition, they might be stopped at sea for interrogation regarding what they saw of our launch. In either event, I don't want to risk running my conning tower into the stern of the tanker while it slows or changes course.

We head for the ocean bottom near a sunken tanker and wait. We seal the battery room, and I order the use of electricity be minimized. The crew whispers in mixed emotions. They are proud of their part in the attack. But they are apprehensive. They know we will have a difficult time escaping to the relative safety of the Gulf of Oman. We will soon need all their skill in addition to a lot of luck. They have also counted the sound from the launches that reverberated throughout the ship. They know that with eight launches we retain unused missiles.

The sonar operators report that the sounds of the tankers' engines grow more distant in their hydrophones. It doesn't take more than four hours until we hear a new surface contact approach. It is the sound of an American guided missile frigate. I suppose in hindsight we should have disabled the remaining nuclear weapons, surfaced, and scuttled the boat. I know that after the American president's declaration, the frigate commander's mission would be to prevent us from launching any more missiles. I figure if the frigate commander knows where we are, they can simply wait for our power and then our air to run out.

The type of patrol pattern used will inform us if we are the subject of a general search to explain a deviation of some measurement used to detect submarines. Alternatively, we may discover a pattern we must interpret as an attempt to pinpoint our exact location. The search pattern transitions to a more specific pattern. I almost believe that we have been discovered. However, the frigate abruptly and loudly speeds away toward the mouth of the Persian Gulf.

If this is a deception, a submarine may have silently moved into the area to wait for us to move. Or there could be a helicopter or aircraft monitoring us at a distance, perhaps monitoring a recently dropped sonobuoy. I don't need to move us out immediately, but an opportunity presents itself. Another tanker is on course to pass near us on a heading toward the mouth of the Gulf. I move us off the bottom. We would intercept the tanker and follow behind and underneath it. The next step after that depended upon our batteries' condition, the tanker's course, or the approach of unidentified contacts.

We emerge from the bottom and intercept the tanker. We venture close enough to the surface to receive images from the UAV. At the point we receive images, we can verify the path behind us is free of surface traffic. We vent the gases from the battery compartment and start our diesels to recharge the batteries.

We raise the communications mast. There is a message from our Ottawa embassy contact. It was dated shortly after the time of the American president's announcement and before we had fired the missiles. It directed both us and *Leviathan* to cease any further attack using nuclear missiles. Of course, the message carries no legal weight to counteract my orders. I don't think I would have made different decisions had I received it before launching our attack.

Avi tells me our sonar computer has detected an unexpected sound pattern. The computer has isolated the sound by filtering out the sound from the tanker's engines. The analysis of the sound against the library of sounds indicates a series of underwater explosions consistent with a pattern of depth charges. Depth charges are used to force a submarine to the surface or destroy it. I had already programmed the UAV to make random ovals around our position to check for surface ships. I reprogram it to take a course that allows us to obtain images of surface traffic in the direction of the explosions.

I break away from the tanker. I keep the snorkel and communications masts extended until we can obtain more information. The UAV provides us with images of several frigates located near the island of Sirri. We can't determine the type of frigate from the visual image. They are moving slowly through or stopped in an area of discoloration and possibly debris floating on the surface. I change the course of the UAV to route it away from the area. Logically, you can say I want to protect it against visual sighting or detection by radar. One side of my brain is happier not knowing any further details, but the logical side of my brain pieces together the explanation. The frigate left our location rapidly. The sonar operators reported the sound of underwater explosions. There were two frigates close together, slowly moving or stopped. The surface near their patrol area featured a discoloration logically associated with diesel fuel. Debris seemed to float upon the surface near the discoloration. The debris represents the remains of *Leviathan*.

The debris is also a sobering reminder to me concerning our predicament. Once detected, our options are limited. Did the frigate give any warning before attacking? Did they attempt to force *Leviathan* to surface before destroying her? Had Jonah attacked the frigate? If so, did he know the nationality of the surface contact?

I know I won't soon receive answers. I can't afford to risk detection by remaining near the surface much longer. I also know that the answers don't affect my decisions. If we are discovered and ordered to surface by the Americans, I'll probably heed their warning. If the Iranians or Arabs discover us, I'm not going without a fight. Hopefully we will sidestep these issues by remaining undetected.

I send the UAV to orbit a position well north of us in the Gulf to act to divert resources to that area should it be detected. We shouldn't need its images; we won't risk raising the communications mast until we transit out of the gulf. I hope the frigates and the rest of that nation's navy will be satisfied that their attack had accomplished their goals. With a bit of luck, they would be too busy investigating the results of the attack to resume a search. I know that even if no specific search for us is undertaken, our presence could still be revealed by sensors and general searches. I plan to move extremely slowly near the bottom. This time, I'll learn from our apparent discovery by a frigate and stay away from shipwrecks. Extra sensors may have been deployed in their vicinity specifically to foil an attempt by a submarine to hide near them.

I turn my attention to making the nuclear weapons "safe" again. The warheads have a sealed core containing both the fissile (nuclear) material and the high explosives that would be used to start the chain reaction. Therefore, our procedures do not involve invading the core to insert material that would prevent a nuclear explosion. Instead, I interrupt the power source from the weapon. I also deprogram the attack routes from remaining cruise missiles.

We develop a small leak, and before the flange is tightened, we put bedding underneath the work area and station a second crewman to catch the wrench should it slip. The bedding gets soggy, but we eliminate any chance the sound of a dropped wrench gives us away. Finally, we clear the Strait of Hormuz.

CHAPTER 14:
OUR BELL GETS RUNG

We make our way to the Gulf of Oman. After we transit to the deeper waters of the Arabian Sea, we rise to snorkeling depth. We raise the communications mast. We read about the American Secretary of Defense's press conference. He answers questions concerning the attack against Iran. The United States wasn't responsible for the attack. He didn't know which nation was responsible for the attack. He believes that all attacks were initiated before word of the president's announcement spread. He would not answer the question of whether the delivery of the weapons employed missiles or aircraft.

The United States wouldn't change the disposition or duties of their armed forces in response to the attack against Iran. The United States would offer disaster assistance to Iran through other nations but not personnel. There is no mention of any military action in the Persian Gulf. The other news includes word of closing of Israel's Paris embassy. Reports confirm the voluntary "relocation" of French Jews out of France's major cities. The relocation represents the government's efforts to protect the Jews from attacks by militant Muslims.

There is a signoff message in the Paris military attachés

mailbox confirming the "relocation." The application of the protective relocation sounds much more pessimistic in tone than the news report. *Leviathan* remains unaccounted for.

We submerge but operate at a fairly shallow depth. I finish reading a message from our Ottawa embassy contact. It says there is "considerable" Pakistani influence upon French domestic and military policy.

Tal, on duty at his sonar station, informs us that a helicopter is approaching. It is dipping its sonar in the water near us. I order the crew to submerge the boat, to change our course by 90 degrees, and to increase speed.

He then announces the sound from splashes consistent with sonobuoys.

I order the crew to prepare to launch the SCUTTER torpedo decoy upon the sound of any "splash" from a torpedo. This decoy is self-propelled and can be launched from our submarine signal ejector. It would automatically activate after launch. It is programmed to listen for and analyze torpedo transmissions and then select the appropriate signal to seduce the torpedo. The decoy has enough propellant to maneuver for ten minutes. The decoy would give off signals that would make any torpedo prefer it to our boat for this entire period.

If the decoy functions according to the promises the designers would have us believe, we should be able to wait until we hear a torpedo hit the water and still benefit from the device's protection.

I'm comparing our predicament to that of *Leviathan*. We are in much deeper water, and our detection here is much more distant both in time and location from our time and place of launch. *Leviathan* may have been attacked from surface ships. The destroyer or frigate that launched the helicopter should remain at a distance.

My thoughts are interrupted by Tal shouting, "Splash. Torpedo!"

We launch the decoy immediately.

Then comes, "Confirmed: torpedo and it is active."

Do you remember the phrase, "Close only counts in dancing, horseshoes, and hand grenades"? Let me add explosives and submarines to the list. We can't even make half the speed of the torpedo. However, if the decoy works according to design, we should be at a safe distance when it explodes. There were several variables: Would the decoy seduce the torpedo, occupy the guidance program for many minutes, and then trigger its detonator? If so, how far away could we travel by that time, considering our need to move slowly enough to not make out detection easy and to preserve our batteries' charge? The helicopter might have moved only a short distance before dropping its torpedo in the water. The torpedo would not need to travel a great distance before it armed itself.

I'm waiting for a report of the distance and direction of the torpedo and whether it is going after the decoy before I decide upon other course changes.

Have you ever experienced one of those moments where everything happens in slow motion? Have you experienced seeing highlights of your life's events passing through your mind in a few seconds?

Both sonar operators scream out in their unique way and rip off the hydrophones from their head.

In slow motion, I witness the other crewmen in the area tighten their grasp on the secure surface of the interior of the boat they have selected for their handhold. I look for something to grab and spread my legs into a stance resembling that of a boxer. Images from funerals I've attended pass through my head.

Just as there is no form of training to prepare an infantryman for the experience of receiving a gunshot wound, we do not undergo realistic training that enables us to experience the effects of detonation of a torpedo or depth charge near the boat. We only train to manage the new hazards its aftermath creates. The shockwave from the blast is thus a new experience for each of us.

The interior of *Tekumah* is now a mess. All unsecured objects and some secured equipment are thrown about the boat. Leaks materialize. The distress level of the crew on duty with me on the bridge ranges from moderate to substantial. The pressure against our eardrums is deafening and disorienting. The explosion has considerable effect upon our ability to communicate and focus at responding to this emergency.

The leaks we have to control are considerably smaller than those created for training purposes since the first weeks of submarine school. The difference is the effect of the panic. The practice leaks are limited and controlled. No submarine trainee has ever drowned in the attempt to control a leak or lost a submarine in the midst of training. Eventually, the effects of repetitive training take over. The leaks are controlled sufficiently so that information regarding other damage can be gathered and forwarded to me.

I suppose the best way to summarize the damage is to report that German machinery is a lot tougher than Israeli flesh. The damage to the boat is minimal, but much of crew is bruised; most suffer from hearing loss. More than a few are emotional wrecks. Instead of sedatives, my prescription is having them work on less critical tasks. I assign the men suffering from "torpedo shock" to look for and remedy the damage. They relocate items that might be dislodged by another attack or violent maneuvering. These men move items blocking access. They collect nonrepairable items and sort them into containers for items that may have salvageable components and those that do not. The men put away other items tossed out of their place by the explosion. I emphasize the need for hand signals or written instructions because of partial deafness of the crew. These instructions include an order to minimize the use of electricity.

My job is to review the events and decide upon a course

of action. Out of the blue, we were attacked without warning. Even though the nuclear weapon delivery phase of our mission has passed, my rules of engagement are clear. I am authorized to ward off an attack against *Tekumah*.

Naval helicopters can carry one or two torpedoes, depending upon the type of helicopter and the mission. Helicopters may also be equipped with a depth charge in place of the second torpedo. I doubt it flew from a base from one of the three nations located nearest to our position: Iran, Oman, or Pakistan. It must have been launched from a frigate, destroyer, or aircraft carrier. It might return to the ship for rearmament, or it might deploy its last weapon. Destroyers and frigates might carry a second helicopter. Also, those ships carry an assortment of weapons that could reach us directly. I don't even want to think about how many helicopters and antisubmarine aircraft a carrier might have. Not to mention that they always travel with other ships and submarines. I doubt we are past the worst.

In the short term, I need to evade the threat against *Tekumah*. Our greatest asset is still stealth, compromised or not. I don't know enough regarding the makeup and location of forces deployed against us in order to plan an attack. Our position is fairly distant from the territorial waters of any nation. This fight will play out in international waters.

We now operate at a depth that makes it difficult for us to detect the presence of helicopters. The sound of their engines can only be detected at a close range, depending upon their type and altitude. As if in a chess game, I imagine the moves my opponent is planning next. If I commanded the surface ship, I would order the first helicopter to remain on station and to continue to attempt to track us. I would not order its return to the ship, barring a fuel emergency, until it could be relieved by another helicopter. If I deployed a single helicopter, I would call for help from other resources. I would station my ship at a convenient spot for the helicopter to find. But I would keep the ship out of the submarine's suspected torpedo range unless I had a specific reason to move in closer.

You've watched the Hollywood movies where the submarine faces a relentless attack by a destroyer. The submarine commander needs to convince the destroyer's commander that the submarine has already been destroyed. The submarine commander orders the release of oil, solid debris, or even life-jacketed bodies through the torpedo tube. This trick always fools the destroyer commander into thinking the submarine has broken up, the attack should be withdrawn, and the destroyer must be now commanded in a fashion that makes it particularly vulnerable to an attack by the submarine. I don't want to spoil your movie-watching experience. I will say, unless the items released conclusively prove destruction of the submarine, the submarine's commander is simply confirming his approximate location. I will also advise you that if you destroy a submarine completely, the resulting explosion and trapped air reaching the surface cannot be confused by modern sonar or optical imaging with the detonation of a torpedo or depth charge.

If we release debris, it must be for a purpose other than trying to convince the helicopter pilot of our destruction. While I can assure you *Tekumah* is in some ways a unique submarine, it shares a common identity called a "type" with more than our sister boats. We are a version of the Type 209. The Indian navy operates a version of the Type 209 called *Shishumar* (Ganges River Dolphin) class. Our location puts us within one thousand kilometers of the Indian coast and under 250 kilometers from the Pakistani coast.

A good submarine or destroyer sonar operator with modern active sonar can probably distinguish the difference in sound between the Indian and Israeli Type 209 submarines. I doubt the dipping sonar used by the helicopter, muddied by the noisy engines, would be sufficiently sensitive.

I decide to place a bet. The stakes I risk consist of a few Indian military meal wrappers, the *Mumbai Mirror* newspaper, and the Indian DVDs. The outcome I'm trying to achieve is to have the commander of the operation against us pause to investigate our identity before recommencing his attack.

I've got lots of details to resolve before I can try my luck. I perform a series of float tests. I test the DVDs in the sealed cases and the meal wrappers in some seawater. Then, I recognize the faults in my scheme. I can't realistically send these items to the surface in a trash bag. Submarine and naval trash bags are weighted to avoid providing evidence of the vessel's presence. Even if made to float, I'd have to count on the pilot or other crew member noticing the debris from what would likely be a substantial distance. This scheme to release the debris in the hope of its discovery is too uncertain and indirect.

We Israelis are often accused of being too abrupt or blunt. Sometimes, this is a bad thing. I think I can make it into a positive in this case. I call for the direct approach. We will send a diver to the surface. I have to write a persuasive note. I want the reader to believe we are a disabled Indian navy submarine that has mechanical damage that prevents her from surfacing. I add that our radio communication mast was disabled. In the note, I "order" the attacks to cease at once and immediate medical help be given to our injured crew members. I also request that our navy be contacted immediately with an apology and explanation. I signed the letter using the most common Indian name I could think of, Raj Singh, in the position of "acting commander of *Shishumar*." Then I weather parts of the letter without obscuring its meaning and heavily distort the word *Shishumar* so that only the *Sh* remains clear. That way, provided *Shishumar*, *Shankush*, *Shalki*, or *Shalkul* were deployed in this area and out of radio contact, we couldn't be proven wrong.

I'm hoping the commander or someone higher up the chain would not contact the Indian navy immediately. The four boats could easily be at port or far south or east of our location.

We add five empty Indian military meal wrappers, the Indian DVDs, and parts of the *Mumbai Mirror* we could find to the container with the note.

I know that flooding the compartment the diver is exiting from and opening the door can sometimes be detected by sonar. Even if the helicopter's sonar operator can recognize the sound, he should know we don't carry weapons that can be fired from the torpedo tubes that can harm him. Besides, any launch sound would be much louder. So this event should not cause him to renew his attack. The ship should be distant enough that its sonar operators would be unlikely to perform a high-quality analysis of the sound. I have to trust that the sonar deployed by the helicopter either fails to detect the sound, or that it might not be readily analyzed and determined to represent a threat once it is relayed to the ship.

So Yonatan, one of our better divers, exits *Tekumah*. When he returns, he gives us his report. Following my instructions, he fired a flare gun straight up. Several minutes later, the helicopter pilot approached. Yonatan had reviewed photographs of helicopters and naval identification markings. He was therefore able to determine the helicopter type and look for unique markings, visible weapons, and their attachment points on external platforms. He signaled out SOS using a light. The helicopter crewman pointed a machine gun at Yonatan and gestured him to strip off his scuba gear and approach. Instead, Yonatan dove back to the boat and left behind the transparent container floating on the surface. Hopefully the helicopter pilot would be more curious than cautious and retrieve the package.

Now I know there are a bunch of you that are upset that we would utilize an insincere SOS for our own advantage. I'm sure that for the last few years your voice has become hoarse from your frequent calls to your representatives to indicate your distress concerning the Palestinian use of ambulances in the role of troop and weapons transport devices. I appreciate your loud protests regarding the Palestinian deceptions used to enable attacks against Israeli hospitals, schools, restaurants, and discos. For those of you who kept silent, I suggest that you remain quiet. I want to remind you that our deception is for use against a military force that launched an unprovoked attack against us.

We debrief Yonatan. He identifies the helicopter type as a Lynx. The markings matched those of the French navy. The weapons platform nearest to him was certainly empty, and he thought the one on the other side of the helicopter appeared empty too, but he couldn't be sure. He couldn't read any unit or ship designations on the helicopter.

We consult the books to verify the type of ships that could carry this type of helicopter. We also want to determine whether these ships could carry a second helicopter.

I order the installation of conventional warheads on the missiles and the setting of the parameters on the torpedo for action against a vessel with the keel depth consistent with French ships that could carry the type of helicopter Yonatan sighted.

I send Yonatan back to spy on the helicopter, this time with binoculars in a dry bag. He gives us a report upon his return. He moved to a position where his surfacing would not be noticed. Shortly after Yonatan ascended, one helicopter approached—"armed" with stretchers. After a moment, the other helicopter and its now clearly visible remaining torpedo headed off. Yonatan used a device to track the helicopter's course within a few degrees. He observed it slow noticeably after ten kilometers before dipping below the horizon.

After I hear Yonatan's report, I must decide how to extricate *Tekumah* from the threat of further attack. Naftali remains occupied with damage issues. Rather than interrupt him, I bring in one of our weapons officers, Meir, for help. We need to knock out the destroyer and do it in a way that the helicopters couldn't be used against us. If we launched a cruise missile, it would be instantly detected by both the helicopter crew and destroyer's sonar officer. The destroyer would tie our attack to the subsurface contact they must have already reported to other vessels. Other weapons platforms in the area would join the search for us and know exactly where to start their search. If the destroyer ventures within range, we could launch one or both torpedoes. However, again these would be quickly detected by the destroyer and helicopter crew, especially if the helicopter dropped new sonobuoys after the attack. And again, the attack information would be relayed to other platforms.

We couldn't move from this spot without signaling that our previous communication constituted an elaborate ruse. However, we had to act quickly before the Indian navy notified the destroyer commander that it could account for all its *Dolphin*-class submarines.

I convene a meeting of several officers to create a plan to escape our problems. Meir has an idea of sending a diver using our SDV (swimmer delivery vehicle) to the destroyer or frigate. The diver would carry either limpet mines or the plastic explosives. He would attach them at the point where the propeller shaft meets the hull. We hoped the explosion would breach the seal and allow seawater to enter the ship. If the plan worked, the ship would be unable to move. Also, the ship's crew would possibly be too busy preventing the ship from sinking to plan any offensive action.

There are several difficulties with this idea. First, we have to depend upon the destroyer being at the direction and distance where it last disappeared below the horizon. Second, the destroyer would almost certainly be moving. Interception by the SDV would be especially tricky. Working near the moving propeller shaft and its turbulence would be extremely difficult. Third, the diver has to remain undetected during the approach and operation to attach the mines or explosives. An approach directly from the rear of the ship has the most chance for success but is not foolproof. Fourth, the destroyer would retain the ability to launch its weapons. Fifth, the SDV lacks range for a round-trip. We couldn't plan for a rendezvous. We couldn't endanger our crew by approaching even a disabled destroyer. This would be a one-way mission.

The concept had an important advantage. An explosion aboard the ship without detection of an associated launch would not be immediately attributable to our activities. We would enjoy a greater chance of escape.

CHAPTER 15:
GOOD-BYE, FRIEND

Yonatan isn't the only crewman qualified to perform this mission. There is one individual who is more qualified with explosives and at least one other crewman with superior diving skills. Yonatan's advantage is his fighting spirit. When I acquaint him with our plan, he readily accepts the mission and doesn't need any explanation of the suicidal nature of the mission. He has two ideas to contribute to the success of the plan. First, he wants to take along a cable to disable the destroyer's propellers. Disabling the propellers would make it easier to work. However, once the cable took effect, it would alert the ship's crew. He would have little time to complete the work. Also, in case the explosives failed to blow apart the seal, it would still leave the destroyer unable to move for a while. Second, he wants to bring one of our noisemakers. He would use this to signal us he could not complete his goal. I could approve these requests without hesitation.

Yonatan wants absolute assurance that we will not consider remaining in the area in the hope of his return. He doesn't want us to contemplate his death or capture after he completes or is forced to abandon his mission. So his request for a suicide syringe stems from his desire to spare his crewmates from distraction or disturbing thoughts. We find a way to guarantee its protection from moisture and add it to his provisions.

We review the layout of the French vessels of the type that could carry the helicopter that attacked us. We discuss the details of the attack. Yonatan will use the plastic explosives to attack the shaft seal. He will also plant limpet mines to delay and disrupt any attempt by divers to free the propellers. After several minutes of technical discussions regarding detonators, many handshakes, and numerous bear hugs, Yonatan is off. We figure he should take about an hour and a half before he could locate the destroyer and perform the mission.

In the meantime, we plot a quick series of actions to enable our escape. Once we hear the sound of the explosion, we must suppose a reaction by the destroyer's commander. We presume the helicopter with the stretchers would be summoned back to the destroyer to ferry casualties to other ships or shore hospitals. At minimum, the helicopter needed to return to the ship for reconfiguration with torpedoes or depth charges before it could be employed in any attack against us. We could also expect the helicopter that attacked us initially to be converted for use in ferrying casualties. We would have a choice of whether to launch our weapons against the motionless destroyer. I decide our chances for escape would improve if we called it a day and moved off.

We would also have to figure that the destroyer wouldn't fire her own torpedoes until the crew determined the source of the explosions. We wanted to use that interval to find a location where she or the rest of what was possibly a substantial task force could not reestablish contact with us.

We would head east toward India. There are several areas in that direction with thermal layers and variations in salinity, making precise sound location more difficult. There are also some areas that make our detection by measurement of deflections in the earth's magnetic field problematic. Of more importance, I didn't think that the French navy would be in a rush to fight with "Acting Commander Raj Singh" near Indian coastal waters.

Avi and Tal operate sound-processing equipment that makes use of circuitry to limit the output of their hydrophones. This design spared them from more than temporary deafness when the torpedo exploded while they concentrated their attention to its pursuit of the decoy. They both listen for the sound from Yonatan's noisemaker, his explosives, the destroyer, sonobuoys dropped near us, depth charges, or another torpedo. Instead, they receive an apparent signal from a transducer (underwater loudspeaker) lowered from a cable.

Morse code has not been the international standard for maritime communication for a decade. It has been replaced by the Global Maritime Distress Safety System. I've got to give my opponent credit for maintaining this capability for so long after the use of Morse code has fallen out of favor. It takes our sonar operators a few moments to realize that they hear a message in Morse code and another two minutes until we can find a crew member who can interpret the repeating message.

"Disabled INS vessel: what are your rescue requirements? We are available to provide assistance."

Now I've got a lot of information to analyze. I'm not surprised that the helicopter still knows our location. Most interestingly, INS can refer to Indian Naval Ship or Israeli Naval Ship. So the message can denote anything from "we believe your message saying you are Indian" to "we know you are Israeli."

There really isn't any choice to make. I'm not going to risk either another attack or a rescue that ends with us facing trial for war crimes. We would not give the helicopter crew the courtesy of a response.

I don't know if Yonatan fought the current, opposing divers, or faulty equipment. I do know that sound travels approximately fifteen hundred meters per second in the water. So seven or more seconds after the detonation, our sonar operators hear the sound and give me the spirit-raising news.

We move off a moment after the sound from the transducer stops. Even those of us who are not religious start muttering the prayer for the dead under their breaths in memory of Yonatan.

We have good luck in running into—actually, under a significant storm. I doubt a surface ship task force, helicopters, or light aircraft wanted to pursue us under these conditions. I'm counting upon the task force commander ordering any attack submarines with the group to stay with the main group to help protect it.

We arrive at our interim destination a few kilometers outside Indian territorial waters near Okha. We need to ascend to snorkeling depth to obtain fresh air and to run our diesels to recharge our batteries. We head south along the coast.

We check the news. There was still no mention of *Leviathan*. The Iranian navy had been attacking vessels in the Persian Gulf, the Gulf of Oman, and the Arabian Sea. I think it unlikely that the French navy mistook *Tekumah* for an Iranian submarine in light of our location.

I have a lot on my mind. I fill out the paperwork to nominate Yonatan for a medal. The fact that I don't know where to send the request doesn't stop me from using my best description of his heroics. Additionally, I have to plan a memorial service for him. After that, I intend to survey the officers and men to determine whether they still have the motivation and focus to safely carry on further operations.

I won't give you all the details of the service for Yonatan. I link his sacrifice to a long lineage of Jewish fighters from the Warsaw Ghetto to the present day. We leave messages for him on the hatch cover he used to exit the boat. We also place a book nearby to collect messages to one day send to his family. Ziv approaches the book holding a shirt, which has a periscope view of a surface ship and the words, "Some vessels are designed to sink; others require our assistance." He places the shirt on the book and says, "You did it, Yoni."

CHAPTER 16:
NOT THROUGH YET

Without a trained and motivated crew, a submarine is just so much expensive metal and equipment. I'm not sure the nature of the orders I will receive when I contact our attaché. The prime minister's orders give me leeway to ignore those orders. We have all endured a lengthy ordeal. I need to determine what operations the crew remains capable of conducting.

I survey the officers and enlisted men individually regarding their plans for the future. Even though the direct approach works well for most issues, I remember a story that illustrates why this method doesn't always work. Automakers surveyed potential car buyers regarding the importance of particular vehicle features and characteristics the consumers would consider important when deciding upon their next new vehicle purchase. They heard all about safety and practical considerations. However, when these features were added to vehicles and were highlighted in advertisements, sales did not increase by the expected amount. When the automakers asked individuals what they thought their neighbor considered important in making the neighbor's purchasing decision, the response generated many more comments that emphasized performance and styling. The response attributed to the neighbors revealed the true feelings of the survey takers.

So I know not to directly question the officers regarding their hopes for the final portion of this voyage. I want to avoid hearing them give me a response based upon what they think I want to hear. Instead, I ask what they think the best result might be for a few other crew members I name. When I hear a possible destination or plan from one man, I sometimes solicit feedback regarding it from the next man.

To start the conversation, I often ask one of the officers if he thinks that another crew member would be happy if we sail to the American naval base at Diego Garcia. None of the officers thinks their boat mates want a life at the mercy of whatever the American authorities might provide. Only a few believe the other men might want a chance to sneak into New Zealand, Australia, or some quiet place and start a new life. Most think that the other men consider that, despite what they'd experienced, their service felt incomplete. They express a common theme. They want to remain connected with each other as a crew. They look to help defend the recovery and rebuilding effort in Israel.

I then assess the point of view of the enlisted men. Conventional thought suggests that I would hear a different reaction. Our enlisted men are generally several years younger and have less time in the service than the officers. They have more to look forward to. Many individuals of their age are selfish. But their response is not any different. I suspect their more cramped living conditions aboard *Tekumah* give them a sense of belonging that overcomes these factors. Cynics might say this group merely lacks the ambition to undertake a new life in an unfamiliar position. I disagree. I believe they show great initiative to a higher mission. They want to "keep the team together and free," as one of the younger men explained it.

So I should find an official contact person to report our

intentions and ascertain how we can do the most good. We remain out of direct contact with anyone in Israel. I must contact our embassy attachés for advice.

I draft a message explaining that we have ceased offensive operations. I give them the range of times it would take for us to head up to Eilat. I advise them that to journey to Haifa would require fuel and food and give them an estimate without including the additional time required for replenishment.

I've got mixed feelings regarding where I'd like to take *Tekumah*. The Red Sea leading to Eilat is closer. However, nearly 40 percent of it is less than one hundred meters deep and approximately 25 percent is less than fifty meters deep. It is less than thirty kilometers wide at the Bab al Mandeb choke point. The currents are tricky. To enter the Gulf of Eilat (Gulf of Aqaba on your maps), we have to pass through the Strait of Tiran. The Strait of Tiran, which is merely five kilometers wide, has only a single deep channel that would be practical for us. If we encounter mechanical problems in the Red Sea, we are surrounded by enemies.

I'm thinking it is more likely we'll be asked to proceed around southern Africa one last time and return to the Mediterranean. Of course, a voyage of that duration requires an additional replenishment and increases the chance for new problems to develop.

I receive the answer, and it has a little bit of both choices. Most of the rescue activities are based in the Mediterranean Sea. We are asked to proceed there and assist in the defense of the coastal communities from seaborne attack. But our first destination is the Red Sea to meet with a missile boat to receive rearmament but no fuel or food.

We proceed to the rendezvous point and receive our weapons: two torpedoes, six Harpoon cruise missiles, and a UAV. The Harpoon missiles are similar to the ones the missile boat can fire, but they are encapsulated for underwater launch. We also receive a note that says, "Thanks for lifting our spirits," with signatures sufficient to outnumber the number of men stationed aboard such a boat by a factor of at least two.

Our next problem is obtaining fuel and food. Our Ottawa embassy attaché will contact the South African merchant ship's manager we dealt with earlier. The embassy controls a limited amount of funds available for our mission. All the charitable fundraising is channeled into rescue and recovery efforts.

The final arrangement with the South African businessman includes a cash payment wired from our embassy. It also encompasses an element of barter for the difference in value. You probably don't need to think too long to figure out what our submarine has that might interest a corrupt shipping company. I agree to pay for the balance due upon our purchase of fuel and food in the form of one shoulder fired antiaircraft missile.

On the way down the eastern Africa coast, it is much easier navigation than earlier in the mission. There are few surface contacts, and we enjoy a wide area in which to operate.

I know that our position on the map has nothing to do with the taste of the food we consume on the boat. However, I must report several facts without arriving at a conclusion. Durban, South Africa, has the largest population of Indian ancestral background outside of Asia. Our position was near Durban when a shortage of other food prompted us to use a large quantity of the Indian military rations. The cook who prepared the meals clearly added some new ingredients. He did not reveal his choice of flavor enhancers, but I suspect some form of sweetener. The meal was more flavorful than almost all those we consumed on this voyage, except those few that featured fresh ingredients.

The conduct of business with a man who does not follow legalities is always tense. On this occasion, I know this meeting will likely be the final time we have dealings with each other. The freighter captain must also realize this fact. He does not want our bow and its ten torpedo tubes facing his ship. It does not comfort the captain when I remind him that our tubes could launch torpedoes and missiles that could reach his ship even when ejected from tubes that faced the opposite direction from his vessel. His response is to suggest we permit one of his crewmen aboard who would lock himself in the torpedo room for hours to ensure all our torpedo tubes stayed empty. We would later release him onto a small raft. He would then use his radio to arrange to be picked up and taken ashore.

This idea would not solve the captain's concerns and would create new problems for us. I now know better than to point out to the captain that we could work around these conditions. We could break into the torpedo room and overcome the man if we had the motivation. We could follow the freighter until the man opened the door and then load the torpedo tubes and attack the freighter. It is also dangerous to place a man in a raft in these waters. Even if the captain shows no concern for a member of his crew, I can't be part of a plan that needlessly risks a life.

I also don't want an outsider on board. We should also not remain on the surface for any period longer than needed for the replenishment. I don't want to have to surface to off-load the monitor.

We only make progress in our negotiations once I agree to place a second antiaircraft missile inside the bag he will supply. Apparently, my word still retains some value because the deal is not complete until I also promise not to inform the shipping company manager of the second missile.

Our journey northward along the western coast of Africa starts smoothly. You already know that in a submarine, conditions can change in an instant. Do you remember when I told you earlier that I selected Yonatan for the underwater mission even though our crew included a better diver? The better diver's name is Erez. He is the type of person who doesn't trust the assembly, repair, or owner's manual. The manufacturer doesn't really know the required grade of fuel, viscosity of motor oil, or service interval or procedures the vehicle needs; he knows. Procedures are only necessary when observed or their absence could be objected to by officers. Despite these shortcomings, Erez is both our best diver and our top diesel mechanic.

I was not present during the episode concerning Erez, so I will quote from parts of my report regarding the events. I conclude the events surrounding the incident exhibit an example of the "Swiss cheese" analytical model of accidents because the accident only materializes when all the "holes" line up.

When one of the engines failed to start, the crewman on duty summoned Erez from his bunk to the engine room. He was awakened from a deep sleep, possibly impairing his judgment. He did not stop to change into his fire-resistant suit. Remember, the rules are not for him. In addition, he may suffer survivor's guilt from Yonatan dying in his place. Psychologically, he may have engaged in risky or careless behavior as a form of self-punishment. The crewman on duty reported several failed attempts to start the diesel using a spray of ether. He reported that Erez grabbed a nearby damp rag, probably under the assumption that its moisture stems from prior use to test whether pipe moisture results from a leak and not from ever-present condensation. Erez did not stop to smell the rag or ask the crewman about the nature of the rag's prior use. He put the rag in his pocket, apparently out of habit. He then seized the can of ether and tried to restart the engine. The ether started the motor but ignited a flash fire that singed Erez's hair and scalp. He removed the rag from his pocket and draped it on his head in order to relieve his singed scalp or extinguish any smoldering hairs. The rag he employed for this purpose was not damp from water. Instead, its moisture resulted from absorption of highly flammable solvent. The flames increased in intensity and ignited the nonfireproof clothing covering his upper body. The other crewman, who should have insisted that Erez wear the fireproof suit, should have stood by with a fire extinguisher. That crewman took several seconds to react with the extinguisher. Erez received second and third degree burns, which covered most of his upper body, and lung damage.

You will recall the small crew complement we carry. We don't have a doctor or a dedicated sick bay area on *Tekumah*. Each of us received training in regard to administering first aid to burn victims. A few of us have received more advanced training in specialized areas, but not burn injuries. Our supplies available to treat this type of injury do not extend much beyond sterile gauze and painkillers. We give the best therapy we can under the circumstances.

I suppose if this incident happened during a previous mission, we would call headquarters and request that we break away from our mission. I would have asked them to find out whether an Israeli or a friendly nation's helicopter could ferry Erez to a proper hospital for treatment. I don't enjoy those options. I can't throw away our ability to complete the mission and risk our capture or death.

Erez displays energy and lucidity during the initial hours following his injury. He understands he will have to stay on the boat and so does the rest of the crew. We supply him with painkillers. I raise the oxygen level in the boat—risking further fires—to make it easier for him to breathe. With our missile-firing days over, Sharon has time available to play the role of nurse to Erez.

I don't know if we deserve commendation or blame for our efforts in connection with the medical treatment we provided for Erez. Our ability to prevent and treat the inevitable infections resulting from the tissue damage is extremely limited. I'm certain the drugs are not enough to dull his pain. If someone administered an accidental overdose, it would be easier for him and would provide us with closure. Only the infections that forced him to lose consciousness on the fifth day and ultimately claim his life on the sixth day give us such relief. We are at a point nearest to Luanda, Angola, when we are able to surface in the evening and return his body to the sea.

There is not a long tradition of Jewish burials at sea. Most of the traditions and rules have developed from a time when we lived and died almost exclusively on land. Submariners are great improvisers. The memorial surface is not an exception. A bedsheet receives decorations in the form of a makeshift Israeli flag and wraps Erez's body. A weight ordinarily used to make our trash bags sink, is modified and discreetly attached to his body. I select a group of his closest friends, including Sharon. I start on a religious note. I explain to the participants that what we are doing for Erez is one of the highest "mitzvot" (good deeds) we can perform. It is such an important act of kindness because we perform it even though its recipient, Erez, cannot thank us. I describe the concern he showed for the boat's engines as an underappreciated gift to the crew. I conclude with a military salute.

We submerge, and I write a letter I expect will never be delivered to Erez's family. I praise his service to the boat, the navy, and the nation. I furnish few details of his death. I do specify that Erez died from an accident while operating the equipment he cared for so much. I add his death occurred in association with our boat's critical service to our nation. I provide only a general "waters near west Africa" location for the boat's position at the time of the mishap. I supply the date and time of Erez' death and furnish a more precise location of the point where we returned his body to the sea. I summarize his funeral and include some comments from his colleagues. By leaving out *Tekumah*'s specific location when the accident occurred and the day of the accident, I've prevented the family from having reason to suppose that Erez lingered after his injury.

Sharon is particularly devastated. On an intellectual level, she knows Erez's fate was sealed at the moment of the fire. Emotionally, it is a different matter. She cared for him the whole time without any substantial breaks. She needs rest and distraction for her own good. She spends time in my cabin. But I don't know how much she sleeps. I hope she is numbing her mind with the romance novel or a video game.

I walk to my cabin to retrieve some papers, and I notice she is crying. We haven't operated at communications depth for many hours, so I know it is not news from outside the boat. I close the door.

I ask, "What's wrong?"

She asks, "What does it take to get some kindness out of you?"

"I know you are feeling sorry about Erez. Don't feel bad that we couldn't save him. It would have been a lot rougher for him and the rest of the crew without you being here to help him."

I add, "It is not your fault. He has to take the blame."

"I don't need you to evaluate my performance. I need a hug—unless that threatens to sink the boat," she offers in the manner of both a criticism and a challenge.

I want to know what is wrong so I can fix it. She wants me to tell her that I sympathize with her feelings and to comfort her.

I weigh the harm of a quick sympathy hug in the manner of allowing Sharon to rest her cheek upon my shoulder for several seconds. I conclude there will be no effect upon the boat's ballast and *Tekumah* won't sink.

She approaches and rests her cheek upon my shoulder. She pulls me and shakes without speaking while she sobs. I'm not enjoying my position. I want to fix the problem, but I can't.

"Hug me," she asks tenderly and then sniffles.

I move my arm from its raised position and place it around her upper back. She squeezes harder. I'm thinking of a lot of things but decide against saying anything. I'm concentrating upon the gauges in the background. The boat's position and course are normal. I'm also trying to sense the moment Sharon relaxes her grip on my back or starts to move away so I can release my own arm. Finally, after one extra squeeze of my back, she steps back and strokes the moisture left by her tears on my uniform.

"I'm sorry. I shouldn't have involved you in my problems," she apologizes.

"No. If you have a problem, the boat has a problem," I reassure her.

After an awkward silence, I add, "I had to punch a crewman, once."

My mouth is getting ahead of my brain. I don't want to compare hugging her to the time I needed to terminate the claustrophobic panic of a trainee with my knuckles.

I add awkwardly, "Whatever it takes to fix the problem."

She gives me a funny look while she catches me reverting from the sympathy giver she needs back to the fix-it man.

"I'm sorry for your loss," I add.

She gives me a look that appears to be an attempt to read something from my own expression before she decides upon a course of action. Then she declares, "I'm sure you've got work to do."

I let her know that unless there is something more she needs, I should retrieve my papers. She gives me a final hug, this time closer to my neck, and leaves.

CHAPTER 17:
YOU MUST BE A SLOW LEARNER

W e are in Atlantic waters between the Cape Verde Islands and Senegal when we receive the news in bits and pieces. First, a missile strike has caused death, injury, and damage in Haifa. The attack did not involve WMDs and targeted locations within the city itself, not merely the port. The news reports contained inconsistent civilian casualty estimates with some reporting nearly eighty fatalities. The second part is an attribution of the attack to France. Then, the news reports a statement from the French spokesman who describes the attack as a response to an "unprovoked attack" resulting in the sinking of a French destroyer by an Israeli submarine.

Submarine officers need to retain the ability to think clearly and behave coolly under the sort of unpredictable pressure the duty requires. The job description does not include a requirement that we suppress any hostile sentiments. Submarine duty does require the ability to act independently in response to challenges.

I compare my feelings regarding the attack on the city of Haifa to a fight between individuals. My enemy starts a fight with me. I then gain the upper hand. The enemy targets my grandmother in retribution because she is the "softer" target.

The other officers and enlisted men don't appreciate this news either. Impugning their honor through the spokesman's phrase "unprovoked attack" hurt barely less than their knowledge of the casualties and damage to facilities in Haifa.

In light of our government's failure to reconstitute itself, I retain the authority granted by the letter signed by the prime minister. Any requests from people not named in the letter are "advisory" or merely additional information for me to consider in making my decision concerning retributive attacks.

It is easy for me to choose a French naval base to target for retribution. I select Toulon, the principle French naval base in the Mediterranean. The base is located within a convenient distance from our planned route, and it is an important base to the French. It features a protective breakwater in its harbor that rules out any torpedo attack, but we maintain a large complement of missiles.

The naval base and its warships have substantial defensive systems. I know these systems will be manned. I suppose that the automatic or "wartime" features would be turned off. The same safety procedures that protect an off course sight-seeing airplane from accidental attack might provide an opening for us. We will maximize our chances for success by following several time-tested strategies. We plan a low altitude attack, hoping the radar return of the missiles would blend into the choppy Mediterranean surface. We will program the missiles for near simultaneous arrival at the target. By the time the presence of the first missile signaled the need for defensive action, we hope it would be too late to defend against even the last missile.

Despite what you observe during the manufacturer's demonstrations, missiles don't always hit the bull's eye. The missile is equipped with a sea attack program that helps it find a ship operating on the open water. It also has a land attack feature to help it locate buildings, for example, aircraft hangers. Both modes are poorly suited to attacking a moored ship. The "clutter" of the dock and port buildings makes it difficult for the sea attack program to pick out the ship's profile. The land attack mode lacks the precision required to make an accurate hit unless you can employ an aircraft equipped with a television link to the missile. So the missile's targeting system requires modification if we expect it to acquire a moored ship.

The portion of the program Sharon modified earlier was less complex than the changes we must make here in order to accomplish our attack. She remains eager to proceed. We first must determine the precise dock location where each targeted ship would be moored. I couldn't simply request our naval attaché in Paris ask for the information. I remember that the Japanese government employed agents in Pearl Harbor who reported the layout of American naval ships in the harbor. I wish I could employ an Israeli equivalent. Sharon handles gathering this data as well.

I told you before that sometimes the direct method is the best way to accomplish the mission. Sharon obtains a French e-mail address with a username that loosely translates to "navy history buff." She then e-mails the naval museum at Toulon and asks for information regarding which classes of ships would be in port for our "visit" later this week. She also asks for a list of ships that can accommodate visitor tours this week. She receives a quick response to her questions. The aircraft carrier, *Charles de Gaulle,* is in port along with an assortment of destroyers and other ships. With few exceptions, visitors are not allowed and are permitted only with advance arrangements. This news indicates we do not need to plan our strike to avoid a particular ship in order to minimize civilian casualties. We still need to know the precise dock locations for the attack.

We would use our UAV. It needs to fly within range without detection to provide us with an image we can use to determine the nature and location of the ships. We would next encode the missile with the specific GPS coordinates of the dock mooring the targeted ship. The missile's terminal target acquisition program needed additional data. Sharon would provide an image of the type of ship we would target for the missile's guidance system. We could then specify the impact point for the missile against the ship.

We have computer disks that contain information regarding different classes of ships and their vulnerabilities. We modify the original analysis because it uses the assumption of an attack at sea with defensive systems available. We will enjoy the bonus of disregarding the defensive systems in designating a final approach angle and impact point.

Out of an abundance of caution, I want to ensure our attack cannot possibly damage any areas with active nuclear reactors. The nuclear-powered submarines should all be in protective submarine pens away from the docks. Even if they are not and one of our missiles were to strike the boat, the weapons specialists assure me its reactor would be unaffected by any strike. The only other vessel that housed a nuclear reactor was the *Charles de Gaulle*. The carrier's reactors were housed well below the waterline. They were heavily reinforced. Our weapons specialists are certain our missile's explosive and kinetic power will have no chance of affecting the reactor, even should it trigger secondary explosions.

An aircraft carrier makes a tempting target for several reasons. Even should targeting inaccuracy prevent a precise impact against the designated section of the superstructure, the missile will likely strike another important section of the ship. Also, the heartiness of the carrier is only partially in its construction. At sea, it is the queen bee protected by a variety of other ships and submarines in a task force. This group of vessels does not assist in protection of the carrier when the ship is moored.

However, a docked carrier is less explosive than when at sea. Carriers typically do not tie up at the dock with their complement of aircraft. These are usually flown off the decks to a naval air station before the carrier reaches port. They return to the ship after the carrier is well out to sea. So the flight deck would not be encumbered with aircraft and the volatile fuel and armament associated with them.

Of course, the ultimate temptation for us to target the carrier is that that vessel is the flagship of the French navy.

Several *Georges Leygues*-class frigates were customarily moored at the Toulon naval base. Unlike aircraft carriers, these ships typically keep their helicopters on their deck while in port. But this fact would not enhance damage from an accurate impact of the missile and its 227-kilogram warhead against the superstructure. The helicopter landing zones were situated on small, isolated parts of the deck.

After we pass the Strait of Gibraltar, we make several final decisions concerning our attack. We choose the number of missiles we wish to assign to each target. We establish a place and time of launch. We also compute a provisional series of waypoints. We rule out having the missiles cross the coast away from the port and then attacking from the inland side. We don't possess sufficiently detailed terrain maps to bring the missiles in low over land without increasing the risk of a crash into an obstacle. We also do not have detailed reports of radar stations in the area. So such a path might increase warning time. It also would require an approach closer to the coast before our launch. We want to keep *Tekumah* near the maximum distance from the base permitted by the range of the missiles. A launch from such a distance will enhance our escape chances.

We also determine the best place and time to surface and assemble and launch the UAV. We settle upon the UAV's course and timing of its visit to Toulon to avoid detection. We decided to pass on the chance of trying to recover the UAV after it provided us with targeting data. It would not make sense to send it back to the port to provide an assessment of damage from our attack. We could set it to return to our area to help give us advance warning of surface contacts. However, we plan to dive far below communications depth; we could not receive its signal. We program it to make several orbits near the coast of western Italy, gradually heading south. Radar detection of the UAV would hopefully cause the French military to spend search resources well away from our location. We surface momentarily, and Ziv assembles and launches the UAV without incident.

The UAV makes its way to the harbor, avoiding the traffic from the local international airport. It takes a path that minimizes chances for civilian or military harbor traffic to spot it. We receive images confirming the presence of the *Charles de Gaulle*. It is not moored at a dock but is anchored in the harbor. We program four of the missiles to acquire the carrier at this location. Four other missiles are targeted against the two frigates.

The feeling surrounding this launch is different from our attack against Iran in several ways. It doesn't necessitate the procedures having to do with nuclear weapons. Also, it has more of a traditional navy feel to it. It amounts to an attack against the naval forces of the nation that attacked our own boat and home port. I also felt the reaction on the receiving end would be, in a way, more painful. The Iranian fanatics probably attacked us knowing our response. They undoubtedly calculated that our counterattack would hasten the return of the Twelfth Imam. I don't think French authorities were expecting a counterattack. This strike would likely cause large military, economic, and symbolic damage. But it would not produce a loss of life in the way our attack against Iran did.

I remind myself of some important historical similarities between the events. Both Iran and France were former allies that turned against us. Iran and Israel enjoyed excellent relations until the Shah was forced to flee. France provided Israel with our first nuclear reactor, sided with us in the 1956

Suez crisis, and supplied our armed forces with Mirage fighter planes and many other armaments until 1967. In fact, in 1962, Marseille—located a short distance from Toulon—was named a sister city of Haifa. However, relations with France soured under the leadership of Charles de Gaulle, for whom the aircraft carrier was named.

I don't suffer from second thoughts regarding the need to undertake this attack. I feel our government would have ordered it. It serves as a deterrent to our adversaries who may seek to exploit our apparent weakness. If we could attack France, we retained capability to strike any nation near Israel. It might even serve to warn the French government regarding the harsh treatment of its Jewish population.

You may think we should have come to our senses and not responded to the attack against our homeland. I shouldn't have to remind you that we suffered substantial direct civilian casualties. I also expect indirect casualties would ensue from the closure of Haifa's port to evacuation and resupply missions. Our own attack targets military assets at a time when they should be lightly manned.

Our launch is without incident. We then move south toward northern Africa. We set our course to that area for several reasons. I expect we will be hunted; I don't want to stay close to France, Spain, or Italy, all of which operate capable antisubmarine forces. The hostility of Algeria, Tunisia, and Libya toward Israel does not concern me. What is important is that their military forces do not maintain the capabilities of the European nations.

CHAPTER 18:
NOT QUITE A SURRENDER

We head south through waters of substantial historical significance. Some of the most famous naval combat involving European nations took place above the area we now navigate. Some of the wreckage from these battles rests below us. All the time we hope our stealth prevents our participation in any new conflicts. The crew is overtired from the ordeal, anxious regarding detection, and curious about the damage to the French navy. Surface contacts that should not cause apprehension raise everyone's pulse. There is much conjecture regarding how many missiles have impacted their targets and the level of damage our strike caused. A few wonder how long the ships would be out of action. But mostly the men contemplate the French submarine-tracking capabilities in the Mediterranean. It wouldn't make sense for the undamaged ships and submarines in port to enter the search for the attacker. Even undamaged vessels need to activate crews and to fuel and arm the vessels. If I were the base commander, I would deploy them defensively to protect the base against further attack. Of course, if the decision-making power had passed up the chain of command to a political authority, such logic might be disregarded.

Our bigger concern is the naval forces already deployed in the Mediterranean. French naval forces are likely already operating in the area. Certainly, they could quickly call upon their land-based maritime patrol planes. I'm not sure whether any other nations would join the search. France is not a member of NATO's military command, but they hold a membership in the European Union. I suppose that if our attack achieved its goal, French pride would already be hurting from damage to their flagship aircraft carrier and other vessels. They won't want to appear to require the assistance of their Spanish and Italian neighbors for their protection.

My plan is to run fairly deep and very slowly. We will ascend to snorkeling depth to recharge the batteries after nearly forty-eight hours. At the same time, we would be able to receive radio and Internet transmissions. We could then proceed without ascending to snorkeling depth again until we reached the relative safety of Algerian waters.

The Harpoon missiles used in our attack can be carried by surface ships or dropped from aircraft. I hope that much effort is wasted searching the surface of the Mediterranean for surface ships.

I admit I'm eager to learn about our strike. I'm hoping for the maximum euro amount of destruction. I'm also hoping for the minimum loss of life. I must admit, however, that if our attack reached the officials responsible for the order to attack us, I wouldn't be sending flowers. It doesn't matter if our warheads struck their targets or not. We would keep our remaining missiles in their storage area.

Like Americans, Israelis come from many different backgrounds. Many are from families that have lived in the area before independence. Others are the descendants of Holocaust survivors. A large part of the population descends from Jews expelled by Arab nations after the independence of Israel. There is a substantial group of dark-skinned Jews from

Ethiopia. The immigration to Israel from the former Soviet Union was intended to include only Jews, but a substantial percentage of those refugees admitted were not Jewish. Israeli society includes a wide range of economic classes. Many of us take politics too seriously. And we understandably live life for the moment. If you've ever experienced traffic in Israel, you know that we are not the most patient and polite people.

Our crew-selection process and training builds a cohesive team. The exhausting working conditions and interdependence of our jobs usually keeps potential hostility at bay.

But these are not normal times. So I'm starting to encounter problems maintaining crew unity and discipline. When the men are busy, there are few problems. They remain focused upon their duties. When they have too much time, they turn dangerous to themselves and to their crewmates with their discussions of events beyond their control and facts they cannot learn. I can change the environment by assigning extra work, but this has its dangers too. The men are already close to exhaustion.

There is an even more troubling aspect to the discipline problem. We all recognize that my orders no longer have the same weight of authority behind them. Most of the crew formerly motivated themselves with incentives for promotion, or at minimum, avoiding disciplinary actions. Performance reviews are now the last thing on their minds. Fortunately, following procedures and orders is second nature to them. I haven't had to tell them to undertake an action that they think is unfair or unwise.

The manifestation of the disciplinary issues has so far confined itself to minor transgressions. A few of the men have attempted to persuade the communications officers to check Web sites or even send messages. I am obligated to punish even the attempted violations in this area. What you don't punish, you encourage. One of the men frequently positions himself in the corridor without any apparent purpose other

135

than having Sharon brush by him. He has ignored warnings to stop. To her credit, Sharon has not responded to this interest or made a complaint. Since a rule is not really a rule unless it is enforced, I must impose punishment.

The special officers have split into two factions. Yossi is allied with Noam, and Sergei is allied with Danny. I'm playing submarine psychologist when I say that I don't believe what they are purportedly arguing about has anything to do with the reason they are arguing. I think a lot of this hostility results from guilt that Yossi and Noam harbor from their participation in the prearming of the nuclear weapons. Sergei and Danny probably suffer pent-up anger regarding my decision to omit them from the prearming procedures. Each individual feels they bear the greater psychological load. They envy the participation level of the other two special officers. Of course, they don't directly fight about this. Instead, Yossi's snoring problem now bothers Sergei. Danny claims he can hear music from Noam's headphones. Noam is resentful that Sergei "ratted on" the crewmen trying to use the Internet to contact home.

No crewman has made a physical attack. They have shouted threats and insults. Mostly, I'm playing the role of parent to men who probably acted more maturely twenty years ago when they attended grade school. I don't enjoy many good options here. We don't have boxing gloves or a ring. I'm not going to alter the sleeping arrangements. It would set a poor precedent. I can't put them at separate ends of the boat. I'm not going to give them my psychological theories. I will insist they treat each other respectfully.

I confine my judgments and remedies to only reported problems and not their psychological origins. It is the responsibility of someone offended by snoring sounds to employ earplugs. I'm not going to blame anyone for actions while he is asleep. Music should be quiet enough that others can't hear it. Attempted security violations should be reported.

We are barely outside Tunisian territorial waters near Tunis. I'm resting in my cabin. My imagination is running wild concerning our duties when we return to Israel. I'm hoping that *Dolphin's* crew is intact and able to replace our crew. I imagine myself leading the crew of the submarine, whose name means "renewal," "revival," or "rebirth," in the effort to rebuild Israel.

My thoughts of peace are brief. I'm too much of a realist or a pessimist. I imagine we will receive more weapons, depending upon our projected duties and the availability of the weapons. Once rearmed, I expect to receive orders to continue our patrol.

We still retain six nuclear weapons onboard. Someone has decorated the two longest-range missiles without art but simply the names "Cairo" and "Damascus." Since I've been responsible for initiating the use of these surfaces for artistic expression, I'm not surprised, and I don't feel any reason to take action. In fact, I find a certain pride in noting that our submarine has already struck land targets in Asia and Europe. The crew now threatens Africa with their lettering on Cairo.

I start to contemplate our future. I imagine we are ordered to pull into port to have our diesels serviced, our fuel tanks topped off, and receive new arms and more food—hopefully some of it fresh. But a spy satellite or specific submarine detection technology reveals our location, and *Tekumah* never makes it out of port. Hopefully headquarters realizes this threat. They will find a way to refuel, rearm, and resupply us at sea without detection. Our diesels will have to keep running beyond their designed service interval.

Perhaps our duty won't require us to serve the mission of strategic deterrent platform. Will we be used instead in the role of convoy escort? Patrol boats make a better platform. They are faster and more maneuverable and employ deck guns. Don't misunderstand my point; convoy protection is important duty. The use of a submarine in the role of an escort ship, however, is similar to employing a Ferrari to pull a trailer.

I spend a few minutes imagining an Iranian ship is threatening the convoy. We receive the call and launch a missile, and the threat is eliminated. No—better still—we observe the approach of the threat through our UAV's camera or our periscope. We order them to turn away, but they refuse and declare their intention to sink the ship carrying refugees. We fire a torpedo. The crew spots it, but their evasive action has no effect. The impact ignites multiple secondary explosions providing a fireworks display for the convoy. One of our patrol boats comes by to look for survivors. Only the captain survives. He appears on television to confess his nation's guilt in the original attacks against Israel and Riyadh and his intentions to attack the refugee ship.

I make a to-do list: (1) Voice concerns regarding detection and attack; (2) ask if *Dolphin*'s crew is available; (3) voice issues with duty as convoy escort; (4) ask about replacement mechanics for Yonatan and Erez; (5) inquire concerning commendation and disciplinary procedures; (6) inquire concerning family messaging and reunification procedures; (7) Is nuclear portion of mission ended? If so, can weapons be disabled and abandoned in deep water? (8) Can special officers and Sharon be discharged before we sail again?

I put the list away and drift off to sleep. I suppose I shouldn't have listed Sharon because she enters my dreams. I'm at my parents' house. I'm on leave, early in my training. Sharon is my boss, and she is trying to seduce me while avoiding detection by my parents. I need to use the toilet. My parents' house has a submarine type of toilet full of waste. I try to turn the valves, but they are frozen shut.

I wake up, check the gauges, and walk to the toilet. The door opens and Sharon emerges. One should never be surprised to spot a crewmate on the boat. Where else would they be? However, my face must have divulged an expression of shock from catching sight of Sharon a moment after having dreamed about her.

"Are you okay?" she asks.

"Sorry. Just waking up."

After my turn in the toilet, I take a quick walk around the boat. I join Rami in the engine room. We must ensure our undermanned crew is capable of performing their duties. I then return to drafting the letter based on my to-do list to have it ready before our next ascension to communications depth. I will post it for the Ottawa embassy attaché.

I review potential courses to finish the journey to the waters near Israel. I don't want to operate too close to European or African nations or islands. However, I don't want to select a course that splits the distance between adjacent landmasses. Such a course would be too predictable. I'll move along near the edge of the territorial waters of the North African nations. If any French naval vessels or aircraft follow me, I'll make them operate far away from home and without ready assistance from European neighbors. I'll reject Naftali's idea of bypassing the Gulf of Sidra to save time.

We ascend to snorkeling depth and start our diesels. We first check the navy frequency, which remains silent. I send my message to the embassies through the Internet and harvest our messages. At the same time, Sharon follows my instructions to intercept military chat from nations of interest, including Iran and France. She also "harvests" general news pages, Middle Eastern news pages, including news stories mentioning Toulon. We detect several unknown surface contacts while we recharge our batteries. None of the contacts turns out to be the type of vessel with capability to track or harm us. When what is almost certainly a scheduled Rome to Tripoli commercial flight approaches, I invoke my theory of "the best is the enemy of the better." We submerge after spending barely more than 80 percent of the time snorkeling we needed to fully recharge our batteries. Sharon has harvested whatever Libyan and Egyptian military information she can gather but must forgo the same from Syria and Turkey.

The crew has been waiting in expectation of an announcement regarding the damage to the ships at the French naval base. More than a few wagers have taken place.

I read the news accounts of our attack against the Toulon base. You don't need to be aboard a submarine to know that poop flows downhill. The poor radar operator will receive blame for the damage to the "pride of the nation" plus two other ships. He might be at fault for being distracted. But he might have received poor training. Perhaps his superiors had previously so harassed him regarding previous false alarms that he feared contacting them on this occasion. Maybe he issued timely reports, but delays in obtaining authorization to engage the incoming targets prevented effective action.

The e-mail message I received was more informative than the news reports of the damage. The French government "back channel" communication revealed that they would undertake no further offensive actions against Israel, its ships, submarines, or aircraft. However, they stated that they could no longer guarantee the safety of Jews in France if the attacks against their nation and its vessels did not cease immediately. So in essence, our attack has forced France to sue for peace. The message indicates that the Israeli ambassador to the United Nations accepted the French terms on behalf of all IDF personnel. *Tekumah*'s crew is ordered to remain silent regarding the events connected to the attack.

The final count of the attack is none killed, one injured, and three ships expected to remain out of commission until the second quarter of next year.

Sharon has a lot of work to do analyzing the data we harvested. She wants to determine which nations are trying to find us and what type of assets they are employing.

I give the crew a speech reminding them the fight with France was not one we sought. I inform them that while

France did not surrender or admit defeat, they decided they could not afford to fight us any longer. We still have a fight, I tell them. We must summon all our psychological strength and self-control to maintain a unified and safe crew.

CHAPTER 19:
AN EXCHANGE

We continue heading east. At the next ascension to snorkeling depth, we raise the communications mast. There are instructions from our Ottawa embassy contact. He has now turned into the de facto Israeli military command for purposes of giving us operational instructions.

Dolphin's crew is not intact. He will arrange for two recently retired, trainee, or *Dolphin* crew diesel submarine mechanics to receive assignment for duty on *Tekumah*. We are no longer needed for escort duty. Israeli and other nations' surface ships will perform that duty. Our duty will be to patrol the Mediterranean, armed with conventional missiles and torpedoes. He shares our concerns regarding the potential for an attack against us if we are detected. He will arrange for replenishment at sea.

We should not need to retain special officers since their primary duty of prearming nuclear weapons should no longer be necessary. Additionally, the American "guarantee" of freedom from WMD attack would seem to trump the availability of nuclear weapons as a deterrent value and makes their use by *Tekumah* a threat to Israel. But he understands if I want to retain the special officers for crew unity or other purposes. Otherwise, I may transfer any or all them to the ship during replenishment. They will either be given duty on a surface ship or serve the reconstruction of Haifa. Sharon's fate is in my hands. My contact does not give me any information upon which to make my decision other than the advice that intelligence agents stationed in Israel were generally reassigned to other duties.

Nuclear weapons should not be needed for our mission for the same reasons the special officers could be dismissed. However, since their security on land or aboard other vessels would be more difficult to provide for, he strongly suggests we retain them for continued deterrence and security.

So again I face some choices. I should probably keep our special officers for backup deterrence to the American president's guarantee if we are to house the nuclear weapons. There is minimal risk that I should need their skills to prearm the weapons. It is unlikely that all four—or even three—should be needed. Any two should be able and willing to give their assent. The trickier decision is which two to retain and which two to send home. If I keep aboard the ones that I employed for the attack against Iran, would they be less likely to launch a second time? The Americans used a different flight crew for the atomic bombing of Nagasaki than was used against Hiroshima. Was this part of the reason? Probably, it was not. The flight crew saw and felt the results of the nuclear detonation. Yossi and Noam merely imagined it.

If I release them to other duty, would they turn suicidal if they were not kept sufficiently busy? Will they associate the destruction they will observe in Israel with their own actions? They shouldn't, but they might. Maybe it will assist the recovery of the survivors for Noam and Yossi to recount the story of their involvement in Israel's retribution for the attack. Releasing them and keeping Sergei and Danny enables me to keep the more hawkish special officers. I could be more certain of them following my orders in the unlikely event we should need to use our nuclear weapons. So I'll offload Yossi and Noam. I'll let them know only a few hours before they are to depart. They don't have a lot to pack.

I'm much more torn concerning what I should do with Sharon. Should I ask her what she wants to do? Should I make an effort to determine her duties upon reassignment? Perhaps she can best use her skills on land. I have the authority but not the moral right to keep her aboard *Tekumah*. What are the chances we need to use her data analysis and programming skills? But what are the chances her skills would be needed by the navy or other branches of the IDF? It is true that her presence still distracts the crew, but she appears to civilize them somewhat at the same time. I'll defer making this decision until later.

We continue along the coast of Libya. Shortly before we approach Egyptian waters, we turn northeast toward the northern coast of Israel near Natanya. I inform Yossi and Noam that they are being reassigned. I can sense their disappointment in leaving us and the anxiety that comes with not knowing what comes next. I ask Sharon if she minds staying on the boat. She tells me we might be her closest surviving "family" and that she would like to stay if we can meet one condition.

"You must let me add some curtains to your cabin," she teases.

"You can place curtains on each window in the entire boat," I respond.

The replenishment goes fairly uneventfully. Our food supplies are not the usual quality. I think much of it is from foreign food assistance.

The device used to reenable our weapons is purposely affixed to a heavy piece of equipment. Not surprisingly, it is not carried on the vessel we meet for replenishment.

We take aboard two new men. I give them a quicker version of the interrogation I gave to Sharon. I also inquire regarding their backgrounds. Elad served in the capacity of a mechanic on one of our older *Gal*-class submarines. At least he should be used to these conditions. In fact, he will find the living conditions superior to his former boat. Gavriel is a naval reserve mechanic previously assigned to duty aboard a frigate. I expect him to suffer through the tougher transition to the subsurface environment. Neither individual is wearing the proper submarine clothing the rest of us wear, but we retain a few extras to issue them.

Of course, issuing them uniforms identical to the rest of us helps crew unity. Much more must be done to keep harmonious relations among the crew. Elad and Gavriel replace two crewmen who were well liked while they were with us. After Yonatan's sacrifice and the suffering Erez endured, any of their negative qualities were forgotten. Each mission gives our crew unique experiences that bond the crew. This mission's duration, stresses, and historical importance will make integration of the new crewmen particularly complicated. If I bunk them in the places of their deceased predecessors, it will only serve to remind the crew that Yonatan and Erez are gone. Every question the newcomers ask or comment they make will remind the rest of the crew that these new crew members are not living up to the memories they hold of Yonatan and Erez. I'm also thinking that while Elad should be able to adjust back to these conditions, Gavriel, in particular, should benefit from the support of someone he knows. If I bunk them together, they can support each other's transition. The crew will certainly view them as a pair, even if I separate them.

My best choice involves a little deception. I'll inform Elad and Gavriel first, and then the crew—they will be berthed in the bunks previously occupied by Yossi and Noam. I'll say that in order to fill the position, headquarters required the replacements receive the upgraded housing normally reserved for the officers. The crew might resent this arrangement, but it is better than the alternative.

I have the first chance to hear from Elad and Gavriel regarding their experiences during the attack. Elad was visiting relatives in Nahariya. When the detonations occurred, he initially suspected renewal of Hezbollah rocket attacks against northern Israel.

The rocket attacks had been a regular feature of life for Israelis living in the north for most of the week before the attack. Leftist politicians had blamed groups in southern Lebanon for attempting to sabotage peace negotiations. Their view influenced the Israeli government not to respond offensively on the theory that such a response would be "counterproductive" to peace negotiations.

After a moment, they knew the true nature of the attack. He kept busy most of the first days using his mechanical skills. He helped rescue people trapped in elevators and tried to fix generators and other equipment. All this time, the city residents could not communicate with the outside world. They wondered if the shelling and rocket attacks that followed the nuclear detonations would intensify and whether they represented the prelude to a ground attack from the north. Elad rode a bicycle south to Acre. There he worked converting civilian yachts into lightly armed patrol boats. This "new navy" kept watch for infiltrators and ferried people and supplies along the northern coast. He saw a lot of suffering but didn't want to give me details of his experiences.

Gavriel held a position as a mechanic at the marina in Acre. He tells me he spent most of his nights patrolling the streets and most of his days reinforcing and sealing buildings. Later, he joined Elad and others in modifying yachts into makeshift cargo and patrol boats. He and Elad volunteered together to escape from the horror they witnessed and to "fight back." I have to tell them they are joining us too late to fight back, but that their contributions are vital and appreciated.

They inquire about the men they are assigned to replace. They are proud of Yonatan, and each views himself in the role of his successor. They don't have much respect for Erez and believe that they would never do what he did. Still, his tragic death appears to awaken them to the risks involved in their service. They ask about the other dangers involved in their duties and the quality of the supervision they will receive. I review procedures and rules with them. When I mention Sharon, Elad starts laughing. I notify him that I am serious.

He says sarcastically, "Welcome to the new navy."

The tour goes fairly uneventfully. They both notice that our missile and torpedo storage area is now partially used for extra food storage. I'll let the rest of the crew give them the details of why we house so few missiles. Elad still can't believe we have a female aboard the boat even after he sees Sharon. I give my orders to Naftali to integrate them into the work schedule slowly and under heightened supervision. Then, I'm off to set our course.

It is almost more difficult setting our course now that we are without a long-range destination or clearly defined mission. I want to keep our speed slow to reduce strain on our batteries and to avoid detection. I'm not expecting any more missile launches, so I'll stay nearer the coast than I would if I were assigned a purely "strategic" patrol. I want to patrol near any potential "hot spots" for infiltration or attack. I'm already fairly far north, so we will head to a position near the Lebanese coastal city of Tyre. I'll stay near the coast all the way to a little south of Gaza. Now that I can respond to requests for assistance, I'll rise to communications depth shortly after dusk and shortly before dawn.

The days pass without incident. I still deal with an increasing number of crew morale issues. They express petty grievances that only turn into bothersome issues now that our mission seems unimportant. The crew now resents the drills they once looked forward to for the opportunity to impress me and to demonstrate their competence to the other crew members.

We receive a message that unidentified rubberized patrol boats are harassing relief convoys along the coast of northern Israel. This is the mission I don't really feel comfortable with. We don't feature weapons designed for use against these fast, maneuverable, shallow, low electronic-signature boats. The most I could do is ascend to periscope depth and attempt to give an advanced warning of their presence. But I should avoid operating at such a shallow depth because we are more detectable under these conditions. I reply that we cannot respond due to our position and the time it would take to position ourselves in a location to provide assistance.

Sergei brings me images of celebrations of the great Iranian "victory" over Israel and America. According to the announcer, all the attacks by the United States against Iranian cities have been divinely diverted to deserted areas. So not only don't they give Israel credit for the counterattack, but they ignore the American guarantee against use of nuclear weapons.

I ask Sergei not to let anyone know this information; it serves no purpose. It is simply propaganda to keep the Iranian regime in power.

He declares that nations don't win wars by performing a partial job. He cites examples of how the Arabs always exploited Israel's territorial pullbacks and cease-fires. He loudly informs me that my "unfinished mission" will cost terrible future Israeli casualties. He then walks away, shaking his head in a contemptuous manner.

CHAPTER 20:
A BAD COMBINATION

Elad and Gavriel would not tell me the horrors they witnessed, but they give graphic details to Sergei and Danny. Sergei shares the news regarding the Iranian "victory" celebration. I know this because I eventually confront Danny, who glances at me with "hard" looks every time I walk by.

I operate under the theory that differences can only be cleared if they are aired. I remind him that destroying Tehran would have cost the survivors in Israel. He figures that the president was bluffing. Danny says the president would not have attacked Israel, citing alternative and inconsistent theories involving either domestic political considerations or the risk of harming the "innocent" Arabs living nearby. I admit that we will never know. He is still animated. I remind him that I won't have my authority questioned and that I can arrange for him to be off-loaded if he can't serve under these conditions. I can determine he doesn't want to test my threat, so he holds his tongue and we each move on.

At this point, I should accept responsibility for not relieving Danny and Sergei from communications duties. At least I might have better secured the computers after I noticed their use for unauthorized research. The computer's log reveals searches for the distance between Tehran and various points in the Mediterranean near southern Lebanon and northern Israel. Research was also conducted regarding wind strength and military bases between those points.

Our submarine does not resemble the large American or British ballistic missile submarines, which feature a configuration to isolate the missile and reactor compartments from the crew. We employ rules that limit the crew's access to particular compartments of the submarine, depending upon their assigned duties. The same concept applies to every piece of equipment aboard the boat.

We don't wear radiation badges. Because we do not generate our power from a nuclear reactor, there is almost no chance of radiation leakage inside the boat. The fissile pit, or what you call the core of our nuclear warheads, is surrounded by a sealed box. This box is beyond robust. Still, someone in our navy specified that *Tekumah* be retrofitted with two radiation sensors in the torpedo/missile room and that these sensors connect to the boat's emergency alarm system.

We probably run twenty fire drills for each radiation drill. The chances of a radiation emergency on this boat approach zero. Also, it takes skill to fight fires, and these skills require practice to remain fresh. For a radiation drill, all we do is identify the warhead simulating the source of the leak, load it into a tube, and prepare to discharge it into the ocean. We then evacuate the torpedo/missile room and seal it off before we move to the other end of the boat.

I am not always the person to initiate the drills. I often permit Naftali or one of the other officers to initiate the drill. However, I am always aware of the nature and timing of the drill. This rule is to prevent running a drill at an inopportune time. So when I hear the sound of the radiation alarm, I have three thoughts in rapid succession. I'm thinking the cause is equipment failure or an accidental or unauthorized drill. However, I can't eliminate the possibility of an actual leak.

During most of the drills, I stay out of the way and observe the officers' supervision of the crew's response. This time, I run to the torpedo/missile room to ascertain the cause of the alarm.

I discover the position of the compartment door is closed and locked, sealing the room. It violates procedures to seal the room before we have any report of the cause of the alarm. We try to open it, but it is jammed. My attempt to contact anyone inside on the intercom is met with the sound of activity but no response.

With our small crew size, I can quickly determine who is not in another part of the boat and who is therefore in the compartment, even if their voices are muffled.

I know Sergei, Danny, Elad, and Gavriel are there. I hear bits and pieces of Sergei and Danny speaking in frightened and urgent voices.

"No, this time longer pauses between the seven blinks and the four blinks."

These few words answer some of my questions in a most unfortunate way. My prearming blinking sequence includes seven blinks followed by four blinks.

We have a procedure that enables a successor officer to take the place of the commander during the prearming procedures. The code that enables the substitution for the commander is contained in the commander's safe. The code is enclosed within an opaque sealed container that provides a vacuum. The code goes blank after a few minutes exposure to air. Alternatively, the code can be communicated by the same groups who provide the prearming codes. When the substitution is ordered, the successor must blink the captain's sequence. The prearming device, having received the code allowing for substitution, does not attempt to identify the successor by a scan of his iris.

Did you ever have the automated teller machine "eat" your

bank card when you entered the wrong personal identification number too many times? We have the same protection for our warheads. After too many failed attempts, a mechanism detonates a special charge that destroys the fissile pit's integrity needed for the fission reaction. Whoever possessed the weapon after that time would require access to an advanced laboratory to reconstitute the material into a weapon. This protection might also trigger from attempted physical tampering.

I'm not sure if the antitampering charge employs a design to crack open the core's casing, but that may have happened here. If the antitampering charge destroyed any of the missile's critical components, such as those for arming or guidance, or if the integrity of the nose cone was violated, the missile could no longer be launched.

We have to enter the torpedo room. We could cut off electrical power to it, but those inside could work around the difficulties this might cause them. I call for the torches.

I hear the sound indicating the successful completion of the prearming process. Then I hear Sergei giving instructions.

"Sort by date modified. Scroll down. These are for Toulon. Now here is Iran. This is for Tehran. Edit the code. 'Note out' the code for waypoints. Now save and replace the file in the other subdirectory. Now hit 'load flight path.'"

I had loaded a null flight path into the missiles from the fire control computer minutes after we left the Gulf. The reprogramming to return the flight data back to Tehran bypassed the normal requirement that such data be entered from the fire control computer rather than be entered in the torpedo room. The targeting data for the missile targeted to Tehran remained stored in the missile's computer. They apparently misused the data retention feature, designed for training and testing, to recover the coordinates. They probably removed the waypoints because Tehran lies just within the missile's maximum range from our position off the coast of northern Israel. They did not want to risk having the missile run out of fuel during an indirect route to the target.

"Launch while we can."

"It's closed. Load it."

"Fire it now!"

We heard and felt the sound of the launch.

I order the crew to ascend to communications depth. It is essential that I contact someone who can alert defenses to shoot down the missile.

They complete a second prearming sequence just before I receive more bad news. The nozzle of the torch has been sabotaged. Its tip is closed by epoxy. The valves are also glued in the off position. It will take some time to cut away the obstruction, and the efficiency of the torch will likely be reduced.

They move on to the targeting.

"Copy the code for Tehran for the next missile."

"Now remove the 'note out' for the first four waypoints. Enter these coordinates. Now copy those four lines and paste them below. Good. Now repeat these waypoints another hundred times."

"What time will it be in Mecca when the fuel runs out?"

"I don't know. Time to see if Allah is great enough to protect his most important mosque."

"Yes. Time for them to learn they can't win."

"Good. Now load the flight path."

Since none of the missiles ever held an attack program against Mecca, they apparently modified the waypoints so that the missile would apparently orbit the Mecca Grand Mosque until the missile exhausted its fuel. It did not matter that Tehran was also the final programmed target for this missile.

Naftali comes to me and wants to know what we should do when the crew opens the door.

I've got several things to keep in mind before I answer. I have to presume the radiation alarm triggered for a reason. At a minimum, the fissile pit must have cracked. Perhaps, the missile's nose cone was split open as well.

The bombs are listed under the category of plutonium weapons, but they, in fact, use three radioactive elements.

The plutonium-239 would have converted to plutonium oxide if it were exposed to air. The alpha rays of the plutonium would not penetrate deeply into body tissues. Ordinary gloves should offer enough protection. However, the particles could embed themselves in the lungs if someone inhaled the dust.

The weapons also contain uranium-238. This material is used to surround the core to reduce the number of neutrons that escape the chain reaction. It is also known under the common name of "depleted uranium" and is not toxic enough for me to worry about short-term exposure.

The weapons also use tritium to allow a larger amount of the plutonium to fission before it blows apart. I can ignore its effects as well. It is the same material that is used to make glow-in-the-dark watch faces.

So I know how to answer Naftali's question. He needs to stop the launches without unnecessary exposure to plutonium oxide dust. He needs to kill them quickly.

"Shoot them, Naftali. Use a mask to protect against the dust."

"I'll take my chances with the dust. I've got to be able to see what I'm shooting at. Gilad, I'm going to need your gun."

Most of guns on the boat were locked away in a cabinet within the missile room. I want to continue listening to the conversation from the men inside, so I violate orders and give Naftali the combination to my safe.

He tosses out everything, leaving the safe open, until he finds my pistol and two ammunition clips.

I feel the boat rock again at the moment they launch the missile toward Mecca. They are still debating targets for the short-range missiles when we open the door. They scream at Naftali.

"Why are you protecting the Arabs?"

"We'll be remembered as heroes."

Naftali interrupts their shouts with gunfire. Then, he and the men close the damaged door to the extent it can be shut.

"No, don't weld it shut," he instructs them.

I run to the communications area. The computers and the radio do not operate. I discover the sabotage that disables them. I need to warn the Americans about the missiles so they can destroy them or at least make them understand that the launch was unauthorized.

CHAPTER 21:
SOME OF THIS SEEMS STRANGELY FAMILIAR

I consider using Sharon's computer, but the boat's antenna connection is broken. Also, I can't expect to fire off an Internet message to the commander of the American Mediterranean fleet and expect he will receive it in time to act. I need to make contact faster than an Internet message. We surface, and I climb out with our emergency radio and broadcast a distress signal. We receive a response from an American naval radio operator. I inform him the details of our crisis and request that the missiles be intercepted. The junior officer instructs me to stay on this frequency. I then hear from an apparently higher ranking or at least more-informed radio operator, possibly from a different ship

"There are two that we track. Are there any others?"

"No others."

"What are the targets and waypoints?"

"We believe the targets are Tehran and Mecca via the most direct route. Do you understand that the launch was unauthorized?"

"We copy your statement. Standby."

It takes only a minute until a third voice come through the radio receiver.

"Remain on the surface and abandon your boat into life rafts. Move westerly from your ship. You will be picked up within the hour."

My next decision is easy. I don't have to follow the orders of the Americans. However, given the condition of the torpedo/missile room, there is not much of a mission that could be performed without decontamination. I also am certain that having surfaced and used the radio, we could never regain our stealth.

I supervise the men while they embark on life rafts. When they are all away from *Tekumah*, I retrieve the letter containing my orders and put it into a sealable bag and then inside my pants. The orders are not really secret at this point. I can still destroy them later if I so choose. I guess I'm keeping it for its souvenir value or to prove my actions followed orders made at the highest level. I destroy the coded information, the disks, the computer hard drives, and flash drives.

I've got another decision to make. My orders are to render the nuclear weapons unrecoverable before I either scuttle the ship or allow foreign sailors to board or sink it. The United States is one nation that has no use for our nuclear weapons, and I don't think they would learn anything they don't already know from their design. But I don't want another nation salvaging them if the Americans don't salvage or destroy them. Our charts indicated that the depth is sufficient to prevent their easy recovery. I must enter the torpedo/missile room.

I take a minute to plan my movements inside the room in order to spend the smallest amount of time within it. I've forgotten my advice to Naftali to protect his lungs, or maybe I want to prove to myself that my second in command is not tougher than I am. I pry the door open and instinctively reset the radiation alarm. That buys me only a moment of silence before it sounds off again. I step around the bodies and move to the remaining missiles. One of the missiles, along with much of the room, is covered with a coating of dust and some larger particles.

The nose cone of one Harpoon missile is blown out. Apparently, they were trying to prearm it when the antitampering mechanism triggered. Its remnants reveal markings containing the number one and an inscription bearing the phrase best translated as "Go to hell, Damascus."

I see a piece of paper near the eye-scanning equipment. It is a message from the Israeli military attaché in Rome. It contains the same prearming codes for the missiles as had been provided by the other attachés. But it also contains the code to allow the substitution of the next ranking officer for the commander. I had not seen this communication before this moment. Apparently, either Sergei or Danny was on duty when they discovered the message in the Internet mailbox. They must have printed the message for themselves without informing me of its contents. I would have had no reason to inquire about an additional message with the codes for the missiles, having already received the ones I needed from the other embassies. I don't know if the code was provided by accident or if Sergei or Danny communicated my supposed incapacity. I suppose they managed to memorize my blinking sequence while I performed it before the counterattack against Iran.

I load the missiles with the nuclear warheads attached into the torpedo tubes and force them out of the boat to the ocean floor.

I pause for a moment to consider whether I should do anything with the bodies. I rationalize that it would desecrate the memories of Yonatan and Erez to give any honors to the bodies of these four. Besides, funerals and memorial services are for the living, and there is no one who can attend their services. Really, I'm only trying to avoid further radiation exposure.

I'll allow the Americans to decide if they want to sink or salvage *Tekumah*. I expect it might be of interest to their naval intelligence community, even though I've destroyed the most sensitive information. However, the Americans may not want the association with the weapons platform responsible for so many deaths. I also wonder which port could host *Tekumah*. Most or all non-Israeli Mediterranean ports would not want to host her—even at an American-flagged base.

I'm guessing they will want to sink *Tekumah*. I wonder what effect such a sight would have upon our crew. Again, I want to get off the boat and avoid unnecessary radiation exposure. So I jump into the water and make a short swim to the last rubber boat, which Naftali kept nearby for my convenience.

Aircraft approach and circle us. These are later replaced by helicopters. A while later an attack submarine surfaces nearby. We are motioned to approach their vessel. They first ask if there are any individuals who are not in a condition to swim. After we tell them there are none, the orders start.

"Approach to within twenty meters. Officers first: strip off all clothing and swim to the ladder."

The officers, including Sharon, strip. When she climbs up to the American submarine, I sense the sailors watching are about to have their eyeballs fall out of their sockets. Sharon is singled out of line and is given a blanket. The rest of the officers are immediately taken to the showers and instructed to scrub with an abrasive wash provided. When a sailor sees I am still holding my sealable bag, he knocks it out of my hand and takes it away. I suppose they inspect it to determine whether it is radioactive or constitutes some other type of threat.

The showers on this submarine are much larger than our showers. They can accommodate several of us at one time. It is not lost on the crewmen that Sharon's separation from us and our forced communal shower at the point of a gun has several parallels to the concentration camp experience.

When we emerge, we are given uniforms. They are all

marked with a *P* and the officers have an *O* marking on the side. Mine has a *CO* marking. We are then given radiation badges. Mine triggers quickly. I'm taken to a "sick bay" where a medical corpsman exposes me to a substance similar to tear gas to force mucus from my nose and to make me cough. They ask me the time of my exposure. By telling them, I've saved having my bowels purged. One of the men starts to give me an iodine pill and then is instructed by his superior not to. I'm thinking this might be because I might cough it up, or maybe they think I am not going to live long enough to develop thyroid cancer. Perhaps the source of my exposure from a weapon rather than as a result of a nuclear reactor accident is significant. Then, they change their mind and give me the pill. I think that either they have concluded that the pill would not be harmful, or they want me to think that they are treating me.

I'm sent back to the showers. By now, the rest of the crew has passed through. I'm instructed to scrub for fifteen minutes. I'm told to scour "everything but your eyeballs—and don't be gentle." I take the job seriously, but I admit I'm a little distracted. I wonder about the distillers that retain sufficient capacity that I can take such a long shower. I am also curious regarding the thoughts of the submarine commander upon his receipt of orders to surface during the middle of a mission. I wouldn't mind a tour of the boat, but I don't think one will be forthcoming. I dress, and they give me a new radiation badge.

They ask me whether *Tekumah* is seaworthy and whether her systems operate. They want my assurance that no explosive charges have been rigged. They also want to know the amount of fuel she carries. I think this is an odd question, but I inform them. Is it because they plan to sink *Tekumah* with a torpedo and have concerns regarding the effect of a diesel spill? Or would they try to put a crew in her and take her to a distant port? They would need to decontaminate her first. I ask what their plans are, but they ignore my question.

They take me to meet the commander. He advises that it was good that I called and that the navy destroyed both missiles. "Good that I called," because this notification was necessary for them to destroy the missiles, or "good that I called" because they would have sunk us or attacked Israel had they thought we conducted a deliberate launch, I'm wondering.

The commander won't tell me where the missiles were when they were destroyed, but I can presume from his statement about carrier-based planes being deployed over the debris recovery zone that there was no nuclear detonation.

A helicopter with a stretcher comes to the American submarine. It lowers, and before I can ask, I'm told that the rest of my crew will be evacuated later and join me in Germany. When we pass near *Tekumah*, I catch a momentary glimpse of another helicopter lowering a man onto her deck wearing what I expect is a suit to protect him against radiation.

I'm taken by helicopter to an aircraft carrier. Only minutes after it lands, I board an aircraft that is most often used for delivery of mail and supplies to the aircraft carrier. The catapult launch off the deck is one of the more unique experiences of my life. The plane turns gradually until we head northwest. Along the way, an officer lightly interrogates me while another crewman makes a video and audio record of the event.

The officer addresses me respectfully. He offers condolences for the attack against Israel. He conveys the feeling of his shipmates concerning the attack against Israel. They were upset by the attack and most participated in prayer sessions asking God to speed her recovery. He says that if he had to serve in a foreign nation's navy, it would be Israel's. He suspends the small talk before he divulges his hunger for falafel or gefilte fish. He notifies me that the number of crewmen rescued is fewer than the number usually present on my type of submarine. I give him a reconciliation. He does not ask any follow-up questions.

He looks at his notes and enlightens me with the information, "You had a female on board."

He hands me a picture taken of her on the American submarine, as if I don't know whom he is referring to or in case I planned to deny the facts. I explain in general terms her qualifications and capabilities. Again, he does not ask any follow-up questions.

I could tell this officer conducted his interrogation to gain my confidence and that the real interrogation would come later.

Just before we land, the crew receives a message. When they hand it to the intelligence officer, he asks me to identify what he calls "the atomic nature" of my radiation exposure.

They must not have briefed the crewman with the camera. His lower jaw dropped, and he momentarily lowered the camera.

I answer the questions. During our approach to the airfield, the officer reveals his surprise that I speak English so well.

I decide to play with him a little and answer in my best-accented Arabic, "*Shukran. Ana atkallam arabi shwayya.*" (Thank you. I speak Arabic, a little).

"You're speaking Arabic!" he declares.

"Don't tell my crew."

CHAPTER 22:
AN ODD REUNION

We land at a large military airbase. They drive me in an ambulance to the base hospital. I receive a hospital uniform and a wristband. My door has a sign posted in English and German that reads "No Visitors." There is a guard at the choke point between the cluster of rooms where I'm treated and the main corridor of the floor. He does not pay attention to anything except for the activity in my room. I'm not sure if he and the around-the-clock replacements are there to protect me from attack or to prevent me from performing any mischief or leaving without approval.

I wonder if the tests they give me are more out of curiosity of the effects of radiation rather than to develop a treatment plan. Most of my questions, such as those regarding bone marrow transplant, remain unanswered.

I have a minor obsession to check whether my hair falls out when I move my fingertips through it. It stays attached to my scalp. I suffer persistent nausea, and I'm on the toilet quite a bit.

I wonder if they will offer me a pill with the ingredient from marijuana to combat my nausea. They don't. Instead, they offer me an intravenous feeding and medication. I take it because I hope it will give me more energy for my promised reunion with the crew in a few days.

I receive a quick and monitored meeting with the Israeli ambassador to Germany. I give him my family information with addresses and phone numbers. I also hand him a handwritten list of my recommendations for promotions or honors for many of the men.

Then the serious part of my interrogation begins. They take me to a room that has no windows. I am seated away from the door. I know they have employed this arrangement for psychological reasons. They have put my "back against the wall" and stationed themselves near the symbolic freedom represented by the door. Of course, if they think the absence of windows in the room is going to bother me, then they are especially foolish.

I am asked to recount the events in chronological order. They employ two cameras for the event. From the way one camera operator keeps adjusting his aim when I move, I suspect he records an extreme close-up of my face. I suppose they will utilize slow-motion playback to try to read my face and determine whether I tell deliberate lies.

Two questions are employed more than a few times. "What happened next?" seems to indicate that I offer them more details of the current topic than they require. "Why did you do that?" denotes my poor decision or one that is not supported by facts I have already given.

Many of the questions are very specific. I think that several of the questions are asked solely to test my memory. Others seem of only the slightest potential significance. Perhaps they know the answers and want to determine whether I am truthful. Maybe they are looking for a baseline truthful response to compare with my other answers.

They ask which day and what time of day the events occurred. I don't have the logbooks that would provide the answer. I can easily recall which crew members were on duty at particular stations for certain events. The constant lighting aboard a submarine frustrates any lasting memory of the time of day.

They have a hard time understanding how the impact points against the ships at Toulon harbor could be so precise. I think they are expecting me to confess that Israel has stolen technology from an American defense contractor. They also suspect we must have employed an agent near the base equipped with a laser target designator. Eventually, they conclude I am not going to change my story and they move on.

They are interested in the details of how the "mutinous four," as my interrogator calls them, gained control of the missiles. When I tell them the story of how I allowed Sergei and Danny to remain aboard and bunked them with Elad and Gavriel, they can't believe such a supposedly smart man would do such a foolish thing. Much time is spent asking me to recount the same details back to them. They repeat my statement back to me with slight changes in order to determine if I'll correct their account. I suspect they still don't entirely believe my account of some of the events. Maybe these techniques reflect the sole "friendly" interrogation scheme they received the training to conduct. We have almost completed a full review of the events. They will save the questions about the prime minister's letter until after the reunion.

I'm thinking that my meeting with the rest of *Tekumah*'s crew makes for an unusual "reunion." Most reunions bring together people who haven't seen one another for years, not a few days. Even in their civilian clothing, recognition will be easy. There won't be any news regarding new marriages, divorces, children, or career changes to exchange. This reunion is of a closer group than schoolmates or members of an extended family. There won't be any food or music. The location for the reunion at an American military hospital in Germany is also peculiar. But is it really so strange to meet here if we are only a few hundred kilometers from the boatyard where *Tekumah* was built?

Finally, reunion day comes. A German attendant wheels me into a conference room with windows on all sides. After a few minutes, the crew arrives. They are all dressed in clothing more suited to cold weather than for the current climate. They crowd around me, and then a couple of the men push the table to the side of the room to create extra space. The attendant leaves.

I can't talk to everyone at once, so I "order" them to line up, enlisted men first, followed by the officers. They sit next to me in a chair placed next to my wheelchair. I have only about a minute for each of them. I discover that a destroyer met the American submarine only a few hours after I left the aircraft carrier. The destroyer ferried them to a military base in Turkey, from which point they were flown to Germany. None of them was allowed to tour the American submarine, but they did see the "uninteresting" parts of the destroyer.

Tal carries a box of chocolates. When he hears me tell Avi about my nausea, he leaves the room, still holding the box, and returns empty-handed. Several seconds later, I see an American patient hobbling down the hall holding the box.

Most of the individual conversation centers around what the men will do next. Most want to return to Israel. Several with relatives living abroad want to join them.

Naftali tells me the Israeli ambassador apologizes for forgetting to ask me, in light of my health problems, if I would like burial in the Mount Herzl military cemetery. I remind Naftali that my bad decisions led to the loss of the boat.

"I would be desecrating the graves of those who truly deserve the honor if I were buried in the same cemetery."

"Listen, Gilad, I should have told you. Those guys made unending derogatory comments regarding your failure to target cities. They asked me what I would have done if I were commander. I didn't think they would act on their complaints."

"Don't beat yourself up, Naftali. I decided which special officers to rotate out and how to bunk the newcomers."

I'm thinking privately that the previous executive officer—with all his shortcomings—would have advised me about these facts.

"Tell the ambassador that I would—actually my parents would appreciate it if he can transport my body to Hof HaCarmel Cemetery in Haifa."

The German attendant returns. Boris playfully, but effectively, holds the door to the conference room closed to buy me more time.

The men hurriedly move the conference table to its original position causing the futuristic speakerphone in the middle of the table to slide. When they catch the phone, Avi and Tal notice the buttons on the speakerphone and start reciting submarine movie dialogue, perhaps to buy me a bit of privacy with Sharon.

"Conn, sonar! Crazy Ivan!" says Avi.

"All stop! Quick quiet!" responds Tal.

Others join in the dialogue at the speakerphone before Sharon walks to my wheelchair. I stand to greet her, and she gives me a gigantic squeeze and an extra one just before she releases me.

"See, I told you," Omri says jokingly, moments before he is roughly silenced by elbows to the ribs from those on either side of him.

She tells me she does not know what to do. Part of her wants to return to Israel, but her technology background would allow her to live comfortably in Europe, Australia, or the United States.

I call her closer to me and whisper, "When you washed my sock," I pause to find the next words.

She looks at me and softly says, "It smelled awful. You

should see if they have a specialist at this hospital who can cure your foot odor problem."

Right at the point where my expression changed from shock to relief, she starts laughing and then whispers, "You were correct to ignore my response to your torpedo sketch. It would have caused endless problems."

I can observe the attendant, who is losing the tug-of-war with Boris, show signs of frustration and start to summon other hospital staff. I don't have time to explain that I did not create the torpedo sketch and did not mean for her to retrieve it from my trash container.

She covertly passes me a cell phone, which she has preprogrammed with her own number and advises me to call her in the next day or two. She is going to investigate my prognosis and determine when I will be permitted to leave the hospital. I hide the phone and thank her.

I call an end to the reunion.

The attendant comes in and approaches my wheelchair.

"We build 'em good in Germany, eh Heine?" I tell Naftali.

The crew applauds, and the puzzled attendant wheels me to another room for more questions.

CHAPTER 23:
MY TURN FOR QUESTIONS

They show me a copy of the final page of the letter from the prime minister. They want to know the contents of the earlier pages. They must have destroyed the first pages. Maybe they are going to use an interrogation technique that requires me to believe they do not possess the other pages. Perhaps I left the other pages on the boat.

I've already attended my reunion, so my interrogators don't hold much leverage over me.

I want something from my interrogators before I answer more questions. I want to know what is known regarding the attack against Israel. I want to know how it happened, the level of damage, and their assessment of the source of the warheads and launchers used. I want to know all they know concerning these events.

I'm not after secrets to share. I simply want to know for my own enlightenment.

I can tell I've generated a discussion between the interrogators. They are unwilling to give me information until they hear my story because they don't want me to change my story to fit the facts they are going to disclose to me. So I extract their promises that they will share their knowledge regarding recent events after I finish answering their questions.

I tell them about the contents of the letter. They are careful to use the proper techniques of making me repeat back the information many times. They tell me I've given them inconsistent statements, or they ask me to agree with a different version of my statement they repeat back to me. Once they are satisfied I've got only one explanation of the contents of the letter, they agree to schedule a session where they will give me the information I seek.

It is 2:15 a.m. when they take me to a room where a man I haven't seen before sits on a chair. They have a purposefully indirect approach to giving me information. They don't allow me to ask my briefer, whose back is to me, direct questions. The briefer, whom they refer to under the moniker "Johnny," doesn't address me directly either.

When I ask my question, it is rephrased by one of my interrogators in the form of, "What do you expect the draft report on these events to say in relation to the subject of ..."

The answer always begins with, "Most people with the presently available information would expect the draft report to offer the following explanation ..."

I suppose this method ensures that I'm not asking questions, and they are merely letting me overhear a conversation between them concerning expectations of the contents of some future writing. They can later deny they directly gave me any information concerning these events.

So playing along with their fiction, I can tell you that they expect the draft report to say that the Americans got wind of the Israeli attack against Iran and persuaded the Israeli government to cancel the attack. For canceling their plans, the Israelis were to receive a more comprehensive and effective attack against the Iranian sites and an attempt to overthrow the Iranian leadership. In return, Israel would have to accept, subject to approval by the Knesset, an otherwise unacceptable peace plan.

The attack by the Americans only partially succeeded. Much rubble littered the landscape, and few civilians died. However, the regime retained its grasp on power. Also, because potential targets that would have risked substantial civilian casualties were bypassed, some important targets, including missile storage facilities, were missed. Also, nuclear weapons, even in the form of weapons that would not have caused damage beyond the immediate area of detonation, could not be employed. So several important targets survived the attack.

American intelligence analysis with regard to Pakistan contained many defects. The "strong horse" theory held that the Pakistani government would be strengthened by the show of force by the Americans. The attack against Iran should have shown the power of the Americans to assist the Pakistani government to retain power and increase the pressure against Islamic extremists. A separate report will address the issue of whether the coup would have succeeded in overthrowing the Pakistani leadership, even in the absence of the unrest caused by the American attack against Iran. At minimum, this report would conclude that the attack failed to help the Pakistani government stay in power.

The new Pakistani military and Iranian military engaged in "substantial cooperation" after the attack. The draft report will not provide details of any delivery of materials and technology.

The attack against Israel represented a well-planned joint venture between Iran and their southern Lebanese affiliate groups. A large number of missiles were launched against Israel from southern Lebanon with either "dummy," faulty, or extremely low-yield warheads. The attack plan contained two likely reasons for this step. First, the Iranians wanted to encourage Israel to expend a large percentage of its interceptor missiles and to focus antimissile sites against the threat from the north at the cost of coverage in other areas. Second, the Lebanese groups' consent to the plan required their participation not trigger any substantial retaliation by Israel. The minimal damage to populated areas met this requirement.

The next step was the Iranian launch of a nuclear-tipped missile. Forensic analysis tied the source of the nuclear payload to 1970s Soviet-bloc origin. The weapon detonated at an altitude that caused a substantial electromagnetic pulse. Most electrical circuits, including the communications systems in the area, experienced immediate outages. A low-altitude airburst of a second nuclear weapon followed shortly after the first weapon. The draft report will state that the source of the nuclear material cannot be determined, although an earlier draft reported forensic analysis consistent with Pakistani origin. Again, the missile track originated within Iran.

After these events, rockets launched from Syria, Lebanon, Gaza, and the West Bank targeted government buildings and air bases. Several ground-based "sleeper cells" located within Israel attacked similar targets.

The attacks incapacitated the civilian government because of the death of so many key elected and administrative officials. The attacks also caused a substantial isolation of military units from command elements. Consequently, no recognized authority with the power to order a counterstrike could be found. No line of succession could be established by authorities because of a lack of information. Even if a successor authority figure assumed power, they could not have gathered sufficient quality information to order an effective counterstrike. Further, the successor authority figure would have been unable to easily communicate to surviving military personnel. Even if the successor authority figure could have established successful communications or given face-to-face orders, a lack of accessible and functioning missiles and aircraft prevented their large-scale use. The electromagnetic pulse also damaged equipment needed to repair the damage to aircraft and missiles caused by the electromagnetic pulse. Many of the best qualified maintenance, flight, and missile crews were reservists. They were not on duty at their bases during the attack. The damage to the electronic communications infrastructure prevented notification summoning their return to duty. Although many reservists attempted to report to their units, often qualified specialists were co-opted for less technical security duties.

The draft report didn't cover the level of civilian casualties from the attack, so they couldn't inform me of any information beyond what the news services reported. The news reports grew increasingly gloomy when areas closer to the detonation of the second weapon were surveyed. The evacuees suffering from blast-related damage, burns, or substantial radiation exposure were interviewed regarding their location at the time of detonation. This information, when matched with the absence of evacuees from other previously populated areas, provided a tool to analyze damaged areas. The map produced from the analysis covered central Israel with odd shapes and different colors extending from Haifa to Ashdod, on the coast to Nablus and Bethlehem, on the West Bank.

The attack against Riyadh, according to the draft report, did not result from use of an airborne delivery device and featured a near ground-level detonation. Again, the source of the nuclear material cannot be determined. However, an earlier draft reported forensic analysis consistent with Pakistani origin.

The attack against Iran by *Leviathan* was considered a technical success. The hardware worked well and largely overcame or bypassed whatever air defenses remained after the American attack. However, the target selection could not withstand critical analysis. Several of the targets were already reportedly destroyed by the earlier American attack. The report criticized the overuse of destructive power against targets of limited value under the circumstances. The overall attack appeared to reflect "an emptying of the target bank" that existed the day before the American attack.

Even viewing the Johnny from the rear, I could determine he was evasive and uncomfortable discussing the events surrounding the destruction of *Leviathan*. He fidgeted, squirmed, and tensed up frequently. On its way out of the Gulf, *Leviathan* apparently came too close to an American aircraft carrier battle group. Radio operators attempted to warn her away. Depth charges were employed as a final warning. Either the warning was not heeded, or *Leviathan* responded with an aggressive move and was sunk by the Americans. There were no survivors.

Our attack drew similar praise and criticism to the assault made by *Leviathan*. The out-of-date target selection combined with and lack of any true retributive or political goal outweighed its technical success.

Well, that's the opinion of the draft-report writers, not mine.

The American president would have ignored any Israeli counterattack against Iranian, Syrian, and even Pakistani cities in the initial round of attacks launched by *Leviathan*. After *Leviathan's* counterattack, indirect contacts with the Pakistani government warned that any large-scale attacks against Islamic holy sites or population centers required Pakistan to respond against American interests. So the president's warning functioned to placate the Pakistani government. Our attack, coming after the president's speech, caused much anxiety and tension in the Pentagon regarding whether Pakistan would respond.

The French surface ship attack against us was at the behest of the Pakistanis. A majority of the drafters of the report used the concept of bribery to describe the relationship. A substantial minority favored use of the word "threatened." The French navy's apology to the Indian navy for their mistaken attack proved embarrassing. The embarrassment turned to humiliation, of course. Experts in Toulon proved the sonar information from the submarine contact belonged to *Tekumah*. The French captain faced military discipline for physically attacking the sonar operator responsible for misidentifying the "Indian submarine." His executive officer faced investigation and possible negligence charges. The executive officer ordered the replacement of the entire shift of sonar operators on duty at the time of the Indian distress call. The group called in as replacements had recently ended a six-hour shift. It was this tired group who failed to hear the approach of the diver whose attack caused loss of his ship.

The French attack against Haifa partially served to save face for France but also to impress the Pakistanis. In the context of the recent events, the attack was said to have inflicted only "light" casualties. However, buildings housing Intel, Google, and Microsoft manufacturing and research facilities were substantially damaged. The draft report called this damage "not inadvertent."

The attack against the Toulon base threatened to reignite hostilities between France and Israel after they had apparently ended. However, the performance of the American-supplied missiles and their accurate targeting was singled out for praise. The absence of fatalities from the Israeli attack undermined the legitimacy of a further French attack. The attack against Toulon nearly resulted in the destruction of an Italian airliner and a Greek freighter by French forces in the days following the attack. It took several days until the French authorities could determine the source of the attack. It took several more days for that government to find a way to negotiate the understanding that ended hostilities.

The section of the draft report concerning the actions surrounding the unauthorized missile launches remained a work in progress. Johnny hesitated for a moment and then said it would likely reflect serious "procedural shortcomings."

The draft report would stress the importance of crew

selection. Sailors assigned to a submarine equipped with nuclear weapons should possess three qualities: integrity, intelligence, and vigor. However, if they don't have the first attribute, the other two will turn into an extreme liability.

Of course, the draft would reassure the reader that the superior American naval practices would have prevented such an unauthorized launch. The draft was expected to point to poor crisis management by the commander. It would also highlight the failure to physically disarm and safeguard weapons and missiles and also to poor crew screening and supervision.

So depending upon whom you ask, I'm a mass murderer, an inexpert selector of targets, a dangerous risk taker, a deficient crisis manager, an amateurish supervisor, or a national hero.

CHAPTER 24:
A HOSPITAL IS NOT A PRISON

If I'm supposed to be dying, I don't quite feel like it. I'm weak from not eating solid food and from spending time in the bathroom with illness at both ends of my digestive tract during my first few days here.

I walk into the bathroom and call Sharon. She has imitated your favorite television private detective. She returned to the hospital and overheard a conversation pertaining to one patient, presumably me, which included the German word *kriegverbrecher* (war criminal). The odds are that is nothing more than some idiot's prejudice. However, she spent a lot of time at an Internet café hacking into various diplomatic and military Web sites. When she hacked into the site for French Foreign and European Affairs Ministry, she discovered draft research being shared regarding the legal basis for my extradition. So the end of hostilities between the Israeli and French military did not bind the French not to prosecute me.

She also managed to watch one of the nurses use a logon ID and password to enter data in the hospital's computer. She asked for and obtained the Web site address used by doctors to remotely access the patient records system. Apparently, I'm not in this facility under my own name, and it took her a while to find my records. She eventually sorted the patients by military ID number. When she found a number that fell out of the normal range, she saw what they used to call my "chart." The file indicates that no reliable estimate could be made of the level of my radiation exposure. I receive antibiotics to counter the increased risk of infection from the effects of radiation on my immune system. They are also observing my hands to determine whether I develop any symptoms beyond the mild radiation burn that remains visible there. My temperature indicates I am probably suffering from a mild infection.

Sharon reports some disturbing discoveries. I received treatments that apparently serve no purpose aside from provoking nausea and diarrhea. Possibly, my interrogators wanted me to believe I suffered from a fatal condition. Theoretically, I would not want to die with a lie on my lips and would decide to give honest answers. The premise depends upon the person being interrogated believing they will suffer in the afterworld for telling a lie so close to the time of their death. I doubt my interrogators stopped to think whether their or my notion of God considers a lie to be more significant than my other actions of the past weeks.

Sharon wants to know if I had complained of pain. I had not. The nurses have regularly administered substantial doses of a painkiller with intoxicating side effects. Even if I did not decide to speak honestly in order to speed my passage into the afterlife, my inhibitions were deliberately lowered chemically.

I could only draw one conclusion from Sharon's report. I must leave the hospital before I am kept in custody to face charges for war crimes or answer other charges for the attack against Toulon. But I need to keep taking antibiotics.

Sharon is very proud of what she tells me next. She has recruited most of the crew to help in my rescue operation, but she managed the plan herself. She stole several hospital uniforms by taking them from the cart containing soiled laundry. She took a picture of a hospital worker's badge by enticing the man to pose for her. From that image, she used a "contact" to counterfeit badges with identification pictures slightly too dark for good clarity. She also stole a few pages from a prescription pad and filled the order for more antibiotics.

She has not yet finalized the part of the plan addressing how I will move past the area monitored by the guard. Sharon asks me for information regarding the morning routine I have observed during my hospitalization. Mornings are the busiest time. The staff drop off breakfast and later collect the used trays. Doctors examine patients and make arrangements for patient discharges during this time. The doctors have always finished my morning examination by 7:30, and nurses rarely visit my room before 9:00 a.m.

She is particularly interested to know what time the guards change their shift. I tell her that the guards change their shift at 8:00 a.m.

"Then we have our plan," she declares.

I would start execution of the plan by performing a simulation I'm qualified to make. The guard would hear the sounds of my retching and spilling liquid on the floor. I would have a time range to perform this task between the departure of the doctors and 7:40, provided a nurse would not also hear. Tal is approximately my size, and he will cut his hair to match mine. He would make his way to my room at 7:52 wearing an orderly's uniform and a badge, pushing the bucket and mop needed for the cleanup. Once he entered my room, I would walk into the bathroom, cut off my wristband, and put on another orderly's uniform Tal will smuggle in. I would clip the other badge Sharon created to my uniform.

Tal would also give me a digital recorder with playback. Sharon directed me to develop a script of sounds and dialogue to record. These sounds, when played back in an endless loop, were designed to impede the guards from violating my privacy by forcing open the bathroom door. I would record the sound of the toilet flushing and my own expressions of things such as "Let me finish, please. Hold on, I'm still sick. I can't hear you. Let me rinse myself before I go to the door." I have to have at least three different types of toilet flush sounds and at least seven different phrases.

I would also leave a note in the bathroom, which we hoped could be effectively locked by the use of fast-drying epoxy on the hinges. The note, which Tal would supply, would declare my temporary absence the result of French agents taking me for questions.

"Those online translation programs make it simple to create a note in English that appears to be written by a native French speaker with a poor English vocabulary," Sharon informs me.

At 7:57, taking only the mop, I would walk out of my room past the guard. Sharon would be distracting the guard at that moment—an activity she is qualified to perform. I would also mimic Tal's earlier walk into my room by moving slowly and favoring my left leg.

After the shift changed, Tal would wheel the bucket out of the room. Nothing should appear out of the ordinary to either guard. We planned to meet Rami in the handicapped stall of the public restroom. He would bring civilian clothing for both Tal and me with him. After ditching the hospital gear in a laundry cart, we would leave through the front door of the hospital wearing our street clothes. Rami would also supply bandages for my face to further disguise my appearance. The toughest part should be for me to summon the energy to give the appearance that I am merely another outpatient or visitor.

As with all plans, there are complications and surprises. The doctors finish with me at 7:28, but they stay in the neighboring patient's room until 7:40. Tal has a hard time finding a bucket and mop and has to make do with a large push broom, a small push broom, and no bucket. My shoes are way too big. Sharon proves so distracting to the guard that she must insist that the guard not walk her to her car or the bus stop. I walk into the wrong restroom. Don't ask. The guards change shifts at 8:04 a.m. Tal, in his anxiety to leave at the moment the second guard arrives, almost comes within view of the first guard. He also overacts in his effort to avoid confusion with me. He behaves too energetically compared to the rest of the custodial staff when he leaves my room.

Nonetheless, we all escape through the entrance to the hospital and pile into a nice luxury vehicle driven by Boris. I don't know if our vehicle came to us from keys fished out of a mail slot in the door of a car repair shop, an unlocked restaurant valet key box, or somewhere else. The best feature of the vehicle is the words on its license plates that translate to "consul general." I'm a little too tired and much too happy to wonder if the plates are facsimiles or are the genuine article, liberated from a diplomat's car.

I get a moment to relax in a seat that is more comfortable than any I've experienced since I left *Tekumah*. The supportive seat and leather surface, however, play only a modest role in the comfort I'm sensing. I'm part of an effective crew on an important mission. This time, our undertaking has little to do with national security. We do not jeopardize the lives of our nation's adversaries. Nonetheless, our short-term task is the essential task of any submarine crew's mission. Our goal is to escape detection.

Sharon asks me for my phone. She wipes it with an alcohol-soaked cloth, replaces the battery pack, and places it into a small package already containing her phone with an address of "Chief Custodian, Trans-Siberian Railway, Vladivostok, Russia" and a return address of "Chief Custodian, Eiffel Tower, Paris, France."

"I wonder what will happen if the post office notices I've used a postcard stamp on this envelope," she laughs.

I'm not going to spend a lot of time thinking about whether the package will be "returned to sender" or make it to Siberia "postage due" or whether the authorities will, in fact, track the phones.

Our last mission ended in part because data was not protected against use by unauthorized persons. We will not risk a similar slipup with respect to our electronic footprint.

Sharon leans over to my ear and whispers tenderly, "If I weren't so busy changing my shape to your specifications, hanging laundry from the periscope, and shopping for torpedo polish, I might have found the proper postage."

It takes me a moment to realize her comments stem from the illustrations of rejected birthday designs. Again, this is an instance where the secrecy of data was not properly safeguarded. I did not destroy the images containing the rejected designs before disposing of them in the cabin I shared with Sharon.

Sharon is telling me she knows I engaged in romantic fantasies pertaining to her. I can correct her impression by informing her of the source of the drawings she recovered. My next mission is to analyze whether I should.

ABOUT THE AUTHOR

RICHARD GOLDEN is a Los Angeles native with degrees in law and accounting. He is an analyst and researcher for a major corporation, as well as a husband and a father of two children. His fascination with current events, military history, and high drama led him to write this story. In working on *Depth of Revenge*, he found that geopolitical crises were sometimes perilously close to the scenarios he was penning.

Printed in the United States
217157BV00001B/94/P

9 781440 115257